Bel Demonio

BY THE SAME AUTHOR

Bel Demonio

by
Paul Féval

translated by
John Stebbing & Randy Lofficier

annotated and introduced by
Jean-Marc Lofficier

A Black Coat Press Book

A somewhat abridged version of this book, translated by John Stebbing, was published in 1864 by Ward & Lock, London, under the title *The Woman of Mystery*. This translation restores the integrality of Paul Féval's text.

Thanks to Janusz Prus.

ISBN 978-1-61227-708-0. First Printing. February 2018. Published by Black Coat Press, an imprint of Hollywood Comics.com, LLC, P.O. Box 17270, Encino, CA 91416.

TABLE OF CONTENTS

Introduction

Bel Demonio was first serialized under that title in the newspaper *Le Pays* from 28 June to 16 August 1850. It was then republished in book form in two very slim volumes by Permain under the title of *Beau Démon* later that same year.

This was a difficult time in Paul Féval's literary career. The serialized novel (*roman feuilleton*) in newspapers was on the decline after the Revolution of 1848.[1] Indeed, on 10 July 1850, a new law was passed that taxed newspapers that published serialized novels. At the same time, the publishing industry was itself subject to various upheavals and publishers were shy about taking on new projects.

---

[1] The 1848 Revolution in France, sometimes known as the February Revolution, was one of a wave of revolutions that occurred in 1848. In France, a popular uprising had ended the Orleans monarchy of King Louis-Philippe in February, and led to the creation of the French Second Republic. In the months that followed, the new government steered a course that became increasingly conservative. On 23 June 1848, the Parisians rose up again in an insurrection, which became known as the June Uprising—a bloody but unsuccessful rebellion. On 2 December 1848, Louis-Napoléon Bonaparte was elected President of the Second Republic, largely on peasant support. Three years later, he dissolved the elected Assembly, took the name of Napoleon III and established the Second Empire, which lasted until 1870.

There was, however, one escape route, which Féval, displaying his usual flexibility, did not hesitate to embark on: writing stage plays.

In 1847, Féval had adapted his novel *Le Fils du Diable* [The Devil's Son] (serialized in *L'Epoque*, 16 February-16 November 1846, Chendowski, 14 vols. 1846-47) as a 5-act play performed at the Ambigu-Comique theater, which had lasted 89 performances—a very successful run at the time. Féval had been assisted in this endeavor by his mentor Frédéric Soulié, the author of the classic *Les Mémoires du Diable* [The Devil's Memoirs]. But Soulié passed away in September 1847, and it was Alexandre Dumas who agreed to produce Féval's next two plays at the Théâtre Historique in 1849 and 1850. They were stage adaptations of his own novel *Les Mystères de Londres* [The Mysteries of London] [2] and *Les Puritains d'Ecosse* [The Puritans of Scotland], itself adapted from Walter Scott's *Old Mortality* (1816).

During the same period, Féval wrote several other more minor plays:

- *La Mort de Lord Byron* [The Death of Lord Byron], a one-act play performed at the Ambigu-Comique in December 1847;

- *Le 24 Février* [February 24th], also performed at the Ambigu-Comique in March 1848;

- *Mauvais Cœurs* [Bad Hearts], also performed at the Ambigu-Comique in February and March 1849;

- an adaptation of Féval's *Les Belles de Nuit* [Beautiful Ladies of the Night] performed at the Théâtre de la Gaité in October 1849); and

---

[2] The play was published by Black Coat Press in a translation by Frank J. Morlock as *Gentlemen of the Night* ISBN 978-1-932983-81-4.

- *Le Bonhomme Jacques* [Goodman Jacques], performed at the Ambigu-Comique in August 1850.

None of these were particularly successful, except for *Les Belles de Nuit*, which was produced at the same time as the eponymous novel was being serialized in the newspaper *L'Assemblée Nationale*, from 21 September 1849 to 27 April 1850, with the added benefit that the play was actually rather different from the novel, presenting many scenes not included in the former. In effect, in order to fully enjoy the work, one had to read the book and see the play as well! A clever bit of cross-promotion!

The bloody repression of June 1848 destroyed whatever illusions Féval might have harbored about the Second Republic. For Féval, who had never been much of a Republican, it reinforced the notion that the Republic was a deeply corrupt and hypocritical enterprise, secretly controlled by the occult powers of money and crime. This would deeply influence his future fiction.

The theater not having provided the success that he had expected, Féval returned to strip-mining his beloved Brittany in several Breton novels:

- *Alizia Pauli*, serialized from 27 March to 20 August 1848 in *La Semaine*, collected in book form as 4 volumes by Permain in 1849, is a fairly typical romance taking place near Mont Saint-Michel;

- *Le Château de Crioat*, published directly as a book by Permain in 1848, is another Breton romance novel taking place in 1813;

- *Un Drôle de Corps* [A Strange Body], also published directly as a book by Permain in 1849, is a pro-Royalist historical novel taking place in 1793;

- *Le Jeu de la Mort* [The Game of Death], serialized from 28 June 1849 to 13 February 1850 in *Le Dix*

Décembre, collected in book form as 8 volumes by Permain in 1849-50, takes place in Paris and Brittany, and is a thriller on the theme of the tontine

- *Les Belles de Nuit* (q.v.) tracks down the disintegration and various misfortunes of a Breton family during the 1817-1820 period.

- Finally, *La Fée des Grèves* [The Fairy of the Sands], serialized from 27 June to 23 October 1850 in *La Gazette de France*, collected in book form as 3 volumes by Cadot in 1851, is a historical tale of love sand revenge taking place in the 15th century near Mont Saint-Michel; many consider it Féval's masterwork.

It is within that context that Féval conceived *Bel Demonio*. Instead of being a Briton novel, it was conceived as yet another variation of a number of themes that Féval had successfully used in the past: a Robin Hood-like hero, vengeance for unpunished crimes committed in the past, to which he had added an original element: secret societies.

The first of his works to be constructed along these lines was *Le Loup Blanc* [The White Wolf], serialized in *Le Courrier français* from 23 September to 27 October 1843, collected in book form as 3 volumes by Chendowski in 1844. The eponymous hero, Jean Blanc, is not only a Robin Hood-type who has sworn to force a villain to surrender an inheritance which he stole from its rightful owner, but he is also the masked leader of a secret society, the "Gang of the Wolves." *Le Loup Blanc* takes place in Brittany in the 18th century and features the first masked hero with a secret identity in the history of popular literature. (*The Scarlet Pimpernel* was published in 1905.)

Les Mystères de Londres [The Mysteries of London], written to capitalize on the popularity of Eugene

Sue's *Les Mystères de Paris* (1843), was also serialized in *Le Courrier français* from 20 December 1843 to 12 September 1844 and collected in book form as 11 volumes by Le Comptoir des imprimeurs unis in 1844. Published two years before Dumas' more notorious *Comte de Monte-Cristo*, it nevertheless shares its dramatic structure, featuring an Irishman, Fergus O'Breane, unjustly transported to Australia, who returns to wreak vengeance on his enemies under the alias of Marquis de Rio Santo. There is, however, a twist unique to Féval, which is that Rio Santo doesn't just wish to destroy his enemies, but the British Empire as a whole, embarking on a number of megalomaniacal schemes; he is also the leader of the secret criminal society known as The Gentlemen of the Night.

Féval revisited the Irish/British conflict in a far less lurid fashion in *La Quittance de Minuit* [The Midnight Receipt], serialized in the prestigious *Le Journal des Débats* from 21 January to 17 May 1846, collected in book form as 7 volumes by Chendowski that same year. *La Quittance de Minuit* was a "highbrow" and rather unmelodramatic novel that featured the fight of the Molly Maguires against the British. While it received excellent reviews, making it a critical success, it nevertheless wasn't a popular one, which must have convinced Féval to no longer drop the more sensational elements of his plots.

Indeed, *Le Fils du Diable* [The Devil's Son, tr. As The Three Red Knights], serialized in *L'Epoque* from 16 February to 16 November 1846, collected in book form as 14 volumes by Chendowski in 1846-47 was as lurid as could be. This time, the setting was Germany and featured the conspiracy of the "Three Red Knights" who are attempting to wrest their young ward's stolen fortune from the evil bankers who stole it.

After having thus utilized England and Ireland, Germany, and, of course, France, as colorful settings for tales of revenge and conspiracies, Féval was bound to use Italy on his "European Tour." Thus, *Bel Demonio*.

Andrea Vitelli is cast in the same mold as Fergus O'Breane/Rio Santo, and his Brotherhood of Mercy is patterned after the Gang of the Wolves or the Gentlemen of the Night. At the heart of the plot is revenge for a crime committed with impunity. But if the revenge plot is the engine that keeps the action going, Féval can't hide his fascination for the character of the criminal mastermind at the center of it all, even if at heart he is secretly a hero. In the end, Rio Santo, Bel Demonio and Fulvio must die to expiate their sins for the crimes they committed under their aliases, even if their ultimate goal was altruistic. This is true, to a lesser degree, of Henri de Belcamp who finds redemption for the crimes of John Devil, but still dies at the end. (Or does he?)

By the time Féval arrives at the first Black Coat novel, *The Parisian Jungle* (1863), that schizoid split is consummated: revenge will be left in the hands of André Maynotte, who, like Lagardère from *Le Bossu* (1857), is clearly a hero, and the evil schemes will be placed in the hands of that immortal fiend, Colonel Bozzo-Corona who is thematically the heir of Johann Spurzheim from The Companions of the Silence, but whom Féval made Andrea Vitelli's bastard child.

The circle is now complete and the curtain can rise on the Black Coats.

Jean-Marc Lofficier

BEL DEMONIO

PROLOGUE

I.

Spoleto, an ancient and noble city, is located several leagues from the Apennines and the northern Abruzzo. A branch of the Nera, a small river which has its source in the mountain, enlivens it with the peaceful beauty of its tree-shaded banks, and affords it that freshness which is so important in southern climates.

Towards the middle of the seventeenth century, a period of wars, conspiracies, and gallant adventures, Spoleto had quite a different atmosphere from what it has now. Some days, it was filled with soldiers and mercenaries reminiscent of the black bands of the Medici and Suffolk.[3] At other times, jugglers and their ilk, great

---

[3] Ruthless German mercenaries known as *landsknechts*. Henry VIII paid for up to 10,000 landsknechts to take the field in his cause, but few Englishman joined these companies. Ironically, one Britton who did was Henry's most implacable enemy, the exiled Duke of Suffolk Richard de la Pole, who called himself the "White Rose" and commanded 6,000 renegade landsknechts known as the Black Band who fought for France in the Navarrese War as well as at the Battle of the Spurs (1513) and the Battle of Pavia (1525), where they were annihilated.

nobles, and artists of all sorts, filled its streets,— when the feudal Count, a man of ripe age, whose character was a mixture of the somber and the fantastic, felt an inclination to be joyous, and gave *fêtes* at his little court.

The Count was a Vitelli from the Neapolitan branch, and the Vitellis were, at that time, powerful lords. They were related to the Princes of Mantua, and were cousins of the Mocade d'Avalo, with whom Urban Vitelli had disputed the Marquisate of Peschiera. It well known that, twice in that century, the Avalos possessed the vice-royalty of Naples.

Ercole Vitelli, Count of Spoleto, called himself, in public documents, Prince of Monteleone and Lord of Ascoli, and was one of the richest nobles in Italy.

He dwelt in Umbria, far from his twenty palaces in the Abruzzi, and his rich estates in Naples. This was because a family *vendetta* had pursued him unrelentingly for years, and never allowed him a moment's peace.

Andrea Vitelli, his cousin, was, it was rumored, at the head of a powerful band of loyalists in the mountains, and had sworn an undying *vendetta* against Count Ercole.

In those troubled times, private vengeance was more readily satisfied than it is today.

Our story begins at the close of a spring day in 1640, when the pretty town of Spoleto enjoyed one of those rare days of perfect repose, in which it was agitated neither by the sounds of war nor festival. It was, perhaps, a moment of calm which precedes the storm; for there had been vague rumors of a conspiracy formed by the monk Campanella, the greatest conspiracy artist in Italy during the seventeenth century.[4]

That a considerable band of mountain brigands, under the orders of a celebrated chief named Demonio, had traversed the region, was well known; but their reason for establishing their camp in the gorges of the Apennines nearest to Spoleto was unknown. It was by no means rare, in those days of chaos, revenge and violence of every kind, for bandits to hold a social and political position very similar to that possessed by the corsairs

---

[4] Tommaso Campanella (1568-1639), was a Dominican friar, Italian philosopher, theologian, astrologer, and poet. Early on, he became disenchanted with the Aristotelian orthodoxy. In 1590 he was in Naples where he was initiated in astrology. His heterodox views brought him into conflict with the ecclesiastical authorities. Denounced to the Inquisition, he was arrested in Padua in 1594 and confined in a convent until 1597. After his liberation, Campanella returned to Calabria, where he was accused of leading a conspiracy against the Spanish. Betrayed by two of his fellow conspirators, he was captured and incarcerated in Naples, where he was tortured. He would have been put to death if he had not feigned madness. He was sentenced to life imprisonment and spent twenty-seven years imprisoned in Naples. During his detention, he wrote his most important works, including The City of the Sun (1602). He was finally released in 1626, through Pope Urban VIII, who personally interceded on his behalf with Philip IV of Spain. He then lived for five years in Rome, where he became Urban's astrologer. In 1634, however, a new conspiracy in Calabria, led by one of his followers, threatened fresh troubles. With the aid of Cardinal Barberini and the French Ambassador de Noailles, he fled to France, where he was received at the court of Louis XIII. Protected by Cardinal Richelieu and granted a liberal pension, he spent the rest of his days in the convent of Saint-Honoré in Paris.

who has been granted letters of marque in the time of the Empire. They sometimes fought for, and sometimes against, the Empire, one day for a viceroy or a commander, another for a feudal lord, but always for the party which paid the best.

These bandits were recruited from all the steps of the social ladder, being made up of men condemned to death, criminals who had escaped from prison, men of family who had been exiled, and great nobles who had either ruined themselves, or were discontented with the existing state of affairs.

They were the scourge of taverns, but the flower of fencing halls; they were also the elite of those who had escaped from the galleys.

These roving hordes of mercenaries were, on some days, cherished by the states, and on others, hunted like vermin, their leaders hung at the gallows.

It was all part of the hazards of war!

On the above mentioned day, Spoleto was in a state of the most profound calm—a calm so great that there was not a single person even in the most frequented part of the town, which was a small open space formed by the junction of three almost straight streets, a circumstance rare enough to be mentioned at a time where property lines were rarely straight

Dinner hour had already arrived, and this, together with other reasons it would take too long to explain, and which were connected with the vague terrors often experienced by the populace during those political crises, of which they were always ultimately the victims, kept the inhabitants of Spoleto at home.

The clock of Santa Maria della Piaggia sounded eight.

A window blind on one of the houses on the Place slightly agitated, and a small object, rebounding from the sculptures of the facade, fell upon the pavement with a metallic sound.

Very good eyes, attentively directed towards the house, would have been able to distinguish a white hand stretched though the slats of the Venetian blind.

The little object that had fallen to the ground was a key. A handsome young man, of between twenty to twenty-two years, with long curling hair, emerging from the corner of a neighboring palace, seized the key, and covered it with passionate kisses.

Then he introduced it into the lock of a low door, and disappeared inside.

At the same moment, or very nearly, three persons appeared from the bottom of one of the straight streets of which we have already spoken.

They advanced almost in a line, balancing themselves first on one hip, and then on another, in the fashion of the dandies of the time, and reached the cross-roads almost together.

They were three gentlemen of good appearance, and magnificently dressed; and it was easy to perceive that the elegance of their costume was too great not to have been adopted for some special purpose; for persons of the best breeding were at no time, except when taking part in public ceremonies, accustomed to displaying the richest garments in the public streets. It was only trades-people and *parvenus* who committed such solecisms against good taste.

The three gentlemen, doubtless absorbed in serious thoughts, seemed neither to see nor to hear anything going on around them. None of them were even at first conscious of the presence of his companions. It must be noted, however, that it was a very dark night, and civilization had not as yet invented gas lamps. Our three gentlemen advanced in a direct line towards the house with the closed blinds, and stopped at an equal distance from each other, directly opposite the window from which had fallen the key.

The house that seemed to interest them so greatly was certainly worthy of the attention of an artist. It was a small Italian palace with a flat roof. The facade, which was covered with sculptures, in the style of the Castle de Gaillon,[5] was moreover ornamented with a large balcony, supported by gorgons' heads. Their monstrous heads stretched forth here and there from a charming sculptured entanglement of foliage, flowers, and animals. Some evergreen plants grew from the moldings, and resembled a bouquet of flowers in the head dress of a coquette, and gave to the attractive house that negligent grace which is as suitable to pretty things as to pretty creatures.

A green blind, carefully closed, fell upon the balcony.

Most of the Italian palaces, at the commencement of the seventeenth century, were disfigured by fortified works, which were rendered almost necessary by the manners of the times; and the absence of them, therefore, gave to the charming house of which we speak a very distinctive appearance. It seemed as though, in the presence of this delightful asylum, the scourge of war and devastation had fallen harmless, and that for its sole de-

---

[5] Renaissance castle located in Normandy, the face of which was designed in 1500 by the renowned Italian architect Fra Giocondo. It was removed in the early nineteenth century for and preserved at the Museum of French Monuments in Paris.

fense, it required but the charm of its appearance, as the perfect beauty of some virgins is sufficient of itself to protect them from the assaults of debauchery.

Our three gentlemen were certainly not artists, for they appeared little sensible of the architectural graces of the small palace, and evidently had eyes only for the blind which fell upon the balcony. There could be little doubt that some intriguing mystery was concealed behind that impenetrable blind.

The curiosity of the three persons was speedily explained. Suddenly the blind was raised to the height of the balustrade of the balcony, and a lovely head, one of those female heads, the golden-brown tints of which Giorgione [6] painted so exquisitely, was visible between the iron arabesques of the balcony.

The beautiful creature was doubtless frightened at perceiving so numerous a company beneath her window, for she immediately allowed the blind to drop.

The three gentlemen, evidently disappointed, half turned upon their heels, in the manner of men who have had the door slammed in their faces at a place where they had expected a favorable reception.

The result of this movement was that they suddenly perceived each other, and, as they were mutual acquaintances, they simultaneously uttered expressions of surprise at finding each other under the same window in such bright array.

---

[6] Giorgio Barbarelli da Castelfranco (c.1477/8–1510), an Italian painter of the Venetian school in the High Renaissance, whose career was ended by his death at a little over 30. Giorgione is known for the elusive poetic quality of his work, though only about six surviving paintings are affirmatively acknowledged to be his.

"Why!" said one of them, "that is Signor Pasquale Contarini, if I am not mistaken."

"And how are my dear Cavalier Tiberio Fanferluizzi and the Signor Capitan?" cried Pasquale Contarini.

"Perfectly well," replied the two gentlemen thus ad dressed; "and you?"

"Tolerable, thank you, tolerable; but may the Devil fly away with me if this is not a very curious meeting."

"Well, it is rather droll."

"Very funny indeed," added Capitan, trying to laugh, but only succeeding in making disagreeable a grimace.

The fact was that the three gentlemen would rather have met in any other place, and under any other circumstances. As it was, they silently wished each other to the Devil.

The Signor Pasquale Contarini was a gentleman of some thirty-five or thirty-six years, somewhat damaged by a too assiduous worship of Venus and Bacchus. But, although he had lost the flower and down of youth, he was still sufficiently well-looking; although his nose had been colored by the god of grapes so bright a vermillion that his whole figure seemed illumined by it. The presence of that nose gave Signor Pasquale Contarini a special verve, a *brio*, that was altogether quite unique.

The Cavalier Tiberio Fanferluizzi was not possessed of a similar advantage, but had red and frizzled locks, and a false air of Apollo, of which he was justly vain. Nothing could be gayer or more magnificent than the appearance of Fanferluizzi, covered as he was with knots, bows, and lace, from the shoes to the chin. The most recent fashions of Spain, France, and Italy were mingled in his tawdry colored garments, from which exhaled an odor of civet, amber, and tuberose, which equally affected the nose and the heart. His whole person was, in fact, such a dandy, that his very sword seemed to be a jewel rather than a weapon.

Such not the case, however, with the rapier of the Signor Capitan, which was sufficient to make one tremble at the mere sight its handle, which contained as many complicated bars as the grate of a prison, Its enormous length, and the iron clamor which it gave forth as the Signor Capitan marched majestically in the middle of the pavement, were quite enough of themselves to make many persons die of fright. It was not gold, diamonds, nor silk, which glittered on the person of Capitan, but leather and iron; although on this occasion he had thought fit to temper the ordinary severity of his costume by certain unusual ornaments, which seemed as much in place as garlands of roses on the gate of a dungeon. We must not forget to add that Capitan also sported a most impressive mustache, which was used in Spoleto as a bogy to frighten naughty little children, and which sometimes prevented them from sleeping quietly tor week.

Capitan occupied a post of confidence with the Count Ercole Vitelli; Pasquale Contarini was the son of a Venetian merchant, who had been exiled by the Secret Council; Tiberio Fanferluizzi possessed a dozen castles, and wrote sonnets to the Moon.

Such were the three persons whom chance had brought together at the same hour under the window of Lucrezia Mammone, one of the most celebrated women of the seventeenth century, a century fertile in famous Aspasias.[7] Lucrezia had been, it was said, the mistress of

---

[7] Aspasia (c.470 BC-c.400 BC). Pericles' lover and partner. According to Plutarch, their house became an intellectual cen-

Count Ercole Vitelli, and this reputation rendered her doubly precious in the eyes of such second-rate dandies as Pasquale and Fanferluizzi.

After having exchanged the few words above mentioned, the three gentlemen saluted each other in the manner of persons who take leave with the intention of pursuing each his separate road.

They took, in fact, a few steps, and then returned to the same place, and saluted each other anew, with a fresh appearance of being about to depart.

Some evil genius, some malicious fairy, seemed to be at work amongst them, for a third time they returned to the same place; and this time Pasquale Contarini knit his brows, whilst Tiberio Fanferluizzi tapped lightly on the ground with his foot, and Capitan twisted his moustache.

After a moment's hesitation, Tiberio Fanferluizzi approached Pasquale Contarini and whispered to him with an air of astonishment:

"Are you not aware, Signor Pasquale, that there is a supper party at Salvator's tavern tonight, at which there are plenty of gentlemen and charming girls? Exquisite wines! But you know very well how his cellar is furnished. You had better make haste, for a place is kept for you, and it is seldom indeed that a merry party commences without you."

---

ter in Athens, attracting the most prominent writers and thinkers, including Socrates. Aspasia is mentioned in the writings of Plato, Aristophanes, Xenophon, and others. Though she spent most of her adult life in Greece, few details of her life are fully known. Some scholars suggest that she was a brothel keeper and a prostitute.

"My dear Signor Tiberio," replied Pasquale Contarini, "do me the favor, I beg of you, of taking my place. The guests will certainly have no reason to regret the substitution. Hasten, then, or the supper will have commenced without you."

Fanferluizzi turned his back on Contarini, and scratched his ear. The latter reflected a moment, and then, approaching Capitan, said to him:

"Have you not heard, then, of the duel between Jacopo Maffei and the brave Santañor?"

"Certainly," replied Capitan. "I knew about it long before you, Signor Contarini. When there is an affair of honor afoot in the neighborhood of Spoleto, I am certain to be the first to be informed of it."

"In that case," rejoined Contarini, "you must be aware that it is to take place at this very hour, on the bank of the Nera; is it possible that you are not to be one of the seconds?"

Capitan bit his lip, but speedily recovered his self-possession, and replied with much *sang-froid*:

"If you would like to have the latest news about the matter, by the blood of Christ, I can furnish you with it. The meeting took place this evening at seven o'clock, by torch light, with swords which would not enter that baby scabbard which you carry by your side; and Jacopo Maffei, your good friend, has, unfortunately, had his head slit open to the teeth, may God save you!"

Contarini turned his back upon Capitan, and scratched his nose.

Capitan, seeing Fanferluizzi drawing near to him with the evident intention of making some remark, anticipated him:

"Signor Fanferluizzi," he whispered to him, "there is a *fête* this evening at the palace of our lord, Count Ercole Vitelli."

"I know this."

"But do you know that the noble Maria des Amalfi is to be there?"

"Well? What of that?" replied the handsome Fanferluizzi, at the same time passing his long fingers through the curls of his red hair.

"Signor Tiberio," said Capitan, with a still more mysterious air, "the ladies are more cruel to me than to you, and I have not your marvelous power of taking them in the pleasant nets of love; but if they disregard my sighs, at any rate they are quite willing to accept me as a confidant."

"Poor fellow!" murmured Tiberio.

"Yes; but although it is a part which you would not like to play, I am contented with it; and it is a fact that the noble Maria has recently confided to me, with tears, that she is pining away and dying of love for your lordship."

"Ho, ho!" cried Fanferluizzi, "why should I care? Are there not plenty of other gentlemen?"

"Have some compassion, my dear friend," rejoined Capitan, "and remember Maria des Amalfi is very pretty."

"Pretty enough, I suppose."

"Very beautiful, indeed, and only twenty years-old."

"Twenty-two."

"Good God! Do you mean to give me the lie?"

"Heaven forbid! Let her be twenty, by all means. It's all the same to me."

"By the blood of Christ! You must have a heart of stone! Maria awaits you this evening at the Count's *fête*."

"Very well," replied Tiberio, coldly.

"And you won't go?"

"Perhaps I may; but at any rate, it is not yet time; you can see that the chandeliers are not yet lit in the palace of the noble Ercole Vitelli."

As he spoke, Tiberio pointed to a large building situated at the end of the principal street, and in the windows of which appeared no lights.

Capitan pulled his moustache and made no answer.

However, at the end of a few minutes the blind was again raised, and the charming head of Lucrezia Mammone appeared a second time at the balcony. The fair creature seemed displeased when she perceived the three gentlemen still in the same place, for she made a small grimace, and a second time let the blind fall.

The three gentlemen looked at each other as at first, but without taking the slightest trouble to conceal their ill- humor.

"It is done to annoy me!" murmured Contarini.

"It is an impertinence!" added Fanferluizzi.

"As it is very plain," said Capitan, "that none of us is willing to be the first to leave, I will propose a means of avoiding any quarrel about it."

"What then?"

"Let us draw lots."

"Oh, confound your means," cried Contarini and Fanferluizzi, together.

Whilst the conversation was taking this quarrelsome turn, the situation was becoming critical. A fourth personage, mounted on a black horse, and wrapped in a great brown cloak, arrived at the spot by the middle of the three streets. As the newcomer had excellent eyes, it was not difficult for him to perceive, at the moment when the blind was raised, the charming figure of Lucrezia Mammone; and his countenance gleamed with one of those rays of unvirtuous delight which are apt to lighten up the faces of gallants when they see a pretty woman.

He spurred his horse on, and leaped to the ground as soon as he had arrived at the corner of the place.

When he had fastened his horse to the iron ring placed for this purpose at the corners of all the streets, he advanced with a rapid step towards the palace.

"It seems that there is a large company here," he said on reaching it.

The newcomer was not received by the three gentlemen with much cordiality. Fanferluizzi and Contarini turned their backs upon him; whilst Capitan, with his left hand on the hilt of his sword, and his right on his moustache, measured him with a glance, from the sole of his riding boots to the top of the black feather in his hat.

The stranger did not seem, however, inclined to take offence at this; for he smiled.

He was a young man of some twenty-five years; handsome, well made, and of a wiry form, which betokened muscles of iron. The sun had bronzed his complexion, which was naturally swarthy. He wore a moustache slightly turned up at the end; and when he smiled, he showed between his dark coral lips a set of teeth of the most brilliant whiteness. His expression was at once animated and firm, and betokened frankness, pride, and audacity. At first glance, he might have readily been taken for one of those seekers of adventure who are always ready to risk their lives for an instant's pleasure, and whose audacity is abashed at no peril.

On seeing the three gentlemen turn their backs on him, the newcomer fancied that they were about to quit the spot; and, indeed, he accustomed to seeing people yield to him; so that when he found that the three still remained, he was profoundly astonished, like a man to whom any resistance is inconceivable.

"It seems, gentlemen," he said, with mock politeness, "that we arc all of us resolved to act the sentinel here. Will it please you, for the sake of making the time shorter, to have a little conversation? It is customary, for instance, in a case like this, for each to recount by what singular chance he happened to come to the place of meeting at the same time as the others."

Our three gallants seemed far from inclined to take this pleasantry in good part.

The stranger, however, went on in the same tone of raillery.

"As far as I am concerned, the story will not be a very long one. A matter of business brought me this morning to Spoleto; in a lonely street, I saw a woman who passed before me as a lovely vision. I followed her, and, when I found where she lived, resolved to return this evening. Of course, one always adheres to such resolutions. The evening has arrived, here I am, and I have just caught a glance of my charming vision behind the blind there."

"Sir," broke in Contarini, turning himself suddenly around, "we are in no humor to laugh, and you would much oblige us by going to dream somewhere else."

"There are some persons," added Fanferluizzi, also turning around, "who have no notion of politeness."

Capitan contented himself with giving a prodigious *ahem* while he twisted his moustache, and rolled his eyes in a manner terrible to behold.

"Oh, Oh!" said the stranger, "that is it, is it? Well, I am quite contented that we should argue the matter in this spirit, if it pleases you. Let us draw, two against two, and the affair will soon be settled."

This proposition was not received with all the enthusiasm that it deserved. Pasquale Contarini and the Signor Fanferluizzi turned towards Capitan, as though to ask his advice; but the latter had taken a martial attitude, which was quite suitable to the circumstances of the moment; however, impatience for combat doubtless had rendered him paler than usual.

"Let us draw! Let us draw! By all means!" he cried, while he made his formidable rapier rattle in its sheath, and gave a terrible glance at the stranger, whom it did not seem to frighten in the least.

"By my faith," said Contarini, "a little exercise with the sword is a trifling enough matter; but…"

"But… for the sake of a woman…" added Tiberio.

"And a woman such as her…" continued Contarini.

"For Lucrezia Mammone, forsooth!" muttered Fanferluizzi, with disdain.

The utterance of this name appeared to have the most extraordinary effect on the stranger. He trembled, and his lips became pale.

"That woman—the one who lives there," he asked, with a changed voice, which had no accent of raillery in it now. "Is that woman Lucrezia Mammone?"

"Certainly," replied Tiberio and Pasquale, together. "What of it?"

The stranger suddenly threw his cloak upon the pavement, and, displaying his finely-formed, athletic figure, drew his sword.

"There can be no question now," he said, in quick imperious tone, "of our fighting two against two; for if that woman is indeed Lucrezia Mammone, as you say, it is I alone who have the right to remain here, and to enter her dwelling. Gentlemen, leave at once—or unsheathe your swords!"

Capitan retreated twenty or thirty steps, but the other two were still waffling.

In the meantime, the eyes of the stranger glittered with angry fire, and the point of his sword touched Contarini's lace frill.

When the latter perceived the point of the rapier against his skin, he drew in his turn, and bravely charged his adversary.

The issue of the duel was uncertain; Pasquale soon began to lose ground. The stranger had a long rapier, with a jet handle, which be managed with admirable ease, and which, it seemed very evident, he would soon be able to lodge in Contarini's body. The Signor was forced to step back, deflecting the blows as well as he could.

Tiberio Fanferluizzi, unwilling that his companion should succumb so readily, drew his damascened plaything of a sword, and commenced making energetic plunges at the unknown man.

In the meantime, Capitan looked on from afar, twisting his moustache. He struck his scabbard from time to time, and even half drew his sword; but nevertheless, he prudently remained at a distance.

At one moment, when the stranger, closely pushed by his two adversaries, leaped to one side to be enabled to renew the conflict at a greater advantage, Capitan felt a genuine inclination to take part in it; but he soon perceived that the stranger, in spite of Fanferluizzi's attack, held his ground well; and he thereupon changed his mind, and cried out as loud as he could:

"Gentlemen! I beg you to observe this fact, that Capitan will never be guilty of so shameful and infamous an action as to play a third in an attack on a single adversary."

In the meantime, the stranger, in spite of his strength and skill, would not have been able much longer to sustain so unequal a struggle; and he had just been driven up against the wall, when Lucrezia Mammone's door suddenly opened, and there issued from it a young man of the most charming appearance, with blonde locks which fell in long curls to his velvet collar.

At the gate, a gentle voice said to him:

"Adieu, Angelo; we shall meet again this evening at the palace of Count Vitelli."

The door closed.

Angelo was the handsome lad whom we saw some little time since, picking up the key and entering Lucrezia's dwelling.

He had no sooner stepped upon the Place than he saw the combat which was going on.

A generous feeling of indignation drove the blood to his face; and, without saying a word, he drew his sword and crossed it with that of the brilliant Tiberio Fanferluizzi, whose knots of ribbons and laces were by no means sufficient protection against this new assault.

The character of the conflict was now suddenly changed.

The stranger, freed from one of his adversaries, speedily recovered his advantage, while the young, blond gentleman made such work with Tiberio Fanferluizzi's plaything sword, that that latter forgot all the rules of fencing, and committed offences against them which would have merited the birch in any school of arms in Italy.

Pasquale and Tiberio sustained the conflict for a few moments; but perceiving that the advantage was decidedly not on their side, they took to flight, leaving a few drops of their blood on the pavement.

The formidable Capitan had long since disappeared.

The combat over, the stranger turned towards the young gentleman and gave him his cordial thanks.

"You have nothing to thank me for, sir," replied Angelo, as he sheathed his sword. "You may be able to do as much for me some day."

And, making with his hand a salute as gracious as his person, he disappeared before the stranger had time to ask his name.

The stranger's eyes followed him for a moment, and then, replacing his sword in its scabbard, and throwing his cloak around his shoulders, he knocked loudly at Lucrezia's door.

The door opened, and the stranger, pushing the servant unceremoniously to one side, stepped in.

II. Capitan

In the large palace, which we have mentioned as being visible at the end of the street, and which was soon to be lit up for a *fête*, we must now glance at Count Ercole Vitelli and the woman who attends to his two children, two girls still in the cradle. The Count and this woman were engaged in conversation together.

The Count was a man of about forty years of age, of a stern and wan-looking countenance. The woman, whose name was Mercedes, was a duenna; her face still retained the remains of a beauty which had faded before its time.

They were both in the Count's bed chamber.

"How are the children?" inquired the latter.

"Fiamma," replied the woman, "is as well as possible; but Regina is poorly."

"Fiamma," murmured the Count, "is my cherished child; my heiress. May God grant her a long and happy life!"

"God will grant her a happy life," murmured the duenna in reply, while she involuntarily heaved a sigh.

The Count glanced at her.

"There is something which you to say," he remarked; and then, as the woman hesitated to speak, he added, in brief and menacing tones: "Speak! What is it?"

The duenna trembled.

"Oh, my lord, my lord," she said, "the past is terrible, and I have done all I could to forget it."

"Always these foolish fears!"

"My fears might have been foolish yesterday; but today, God knows, I have good reasons for trembling."

"Explain yourself!"

"I've seen him!"

"Who?"

"*Him*! He whose father and mother…"

"Andrea?"

The duenna shivered, as she uttered, with a faint voice:

"Demonio!"

The Count grew pale.

"It is he, then, who is Demonio," he murmured. Have you spoken to him?"

"Yes."

"What did you say to him?"

"All."

The Count made a movement of uncontrollable rage.

"Wretched woman!" be began.

"Signor," interrupted the duenna, "he is strong, and I am weak. He threatened to murder me."

"And whenever anyone threatens you," muttered the Count to himself, "you always yield."

"Yes. You cannot have forgotten, Signor," replied the duenna with bitterness, "that when, on one occasion, you threatened me, I yielded—to my eternal misery."

"Silence!" broke in the Count. "You have told him that Lucrezia Mammone…"

"I have told him all, Signor, all that has passed since ten years ago. As for that which took place before, Andrea already knew it."

The Count reflected for a moment.

"Go," he said, "and have Capitan sent to me immediately."

The duenna left the room, and almost directly afterwards Capitan entered, smiling and making obeisances.

"My lord wishes to know the result of my mission. I have watched at the Signora's door, and made the following observations. Tiberio Fanferluizzi and Pasquale Contarini were playing the monkey, as usual, under the balcony of the charming lady, but the little Angelo was far more clever, for he went in. Yes, in the Devil's name, if he didn't have the key of the little door by which my illustrious master himself (here, the speaker made a respectful inclination) has alone the the right to enter."

The Count seemed not to have heard him.

"This is not the time," he said, "to speak of love affairs and jealousy; serious danger threatens my house."

"Have you not good swords at your service?" began Capitan.

"Be quiet!" interrupted the Count. "He is here."

"Of whom does your lordship speak?"

"Of whom? Of the man whose return I have so much dreaded."

"Our lost cousin?"

"Yes."

"Andrea Vitelli?"

"Andrea Vitelli."

"The Devil," said Capitan. "And how do you know it?"

"You all say nonsense! Nonsense! But it is the truth nevertheless. Andrea Vitelli is no other than the mountain chief, called Demonio."

"The Devil! The Devil!" repeated Capitan.

"Mercedes has told me all," said the Count.

"Then how did Mercedes find it out?" \

"She was in service in the house of the Countess, his mother. He has introduced himself into my own house—God only knows how—seeking Mercedes, whom the sight of him has driven crazy. She has told him all."

"All, my lord? That's a lot to tell."

The Count sighed and made no reply.

"Ah! The Devil!" muttered Capitan. "It is very plain those whom one does not kill outright are sure to return one day or another. Do you know where to find him?"

"It is for the purpose of finding him that I have sent for you. He's a handsome cavalier, twenty-five years of age, wearing a hat with a black feather, a black doublet, a black mantle…"

"…And a rapier two ells long, with a jet-black hilt?"

"Do you know him?"

"I have seen him."

The Count gestured at Capitan to sit down beside him.

"You are the pearl of my men," he said "Would you like to earn a hundred gold ducats at a single stroke"

"I do not need a hundred gold ducats to serve my master."

"Listen. Our cousin, Andrea Vitelli, must not be allowed to leave Spoleto."

"All right,"

"And the matter must be managed neatly, without fuss, you understand?"

"Perfectly, my lord."

"You will undertake this matter?"

"On my life!"

Capitan rose, saluted his master, and sallied forth in quest of his own men; for the matter he had undertaken was difficult.

The assassin did not lie to himself about the perils attendant on his task. Nevertheless, by using fifty to attack one, he hoped to be able to achieve it with honor.

III.

The small square where the first scene of this story took place had long since been deserted.

The lights in front of the houses burned; and still the windows of Count Ercole Vitelli's palace were not yet illuminated for the *fête*.

The only sounds to be heard were the distant notes of revelry from the taverns in which Capitan was seeking his troops, and the slow murmur of the Nera, flowing twenty paces distant from the gothic mansion, between its two quays, with marble parapets.

The Nera, which flowed round the mansion, traversing its shaded gardens, was, here, wide and deep. From time to time, a waterman passed along its course, singing in his skiff. Then silence fell once more upon the scene.

The door of the gothic house had admitted the stranger, who had gone straight to the mistress of the mansion—a very young woman, wonderfully beautiful, and dressed as though for a *fête*.

Lucrezia Mammone had pearls in her magnificent hair, which formed a framework of jet to her pale countenance. Her form, her supple and voluptuous form, was enveloped in a magnificent satin robe, made in the Neapolitan style.

Lucrezia Mammone, scarcely seventeen, had developed a of figure which women do not attain in France till the age of twenty-five, and which was exquisite in her beauty, that united the most perfect bloom, with all the sweetness of adolescence.

She gazed at the stranger, who held her by the hand; gazed at him with astonishment mingled with fear.

The stranger was Andrea Vitelli. For the space of about a minute, he had been sitting upon a sofa near Lucrezia.

"Look at me; look at me," he said.

"I am looking at you, Signor," said the beautiful girl, "but I do not recognize you."

And then, as the black, piercing eyes of Andrea Vitelli fastened upon her, her eyes fell; and she murmured with a timid voice:

"I cannot tell what it is I feel with respect to you, Signor. When persons enter my presence in the way you have, I have them driven out by my servants; but you—I listen to you, and I obey you.

"Look at me, Lucrezia," said the stranger, again.

"I do look at you, but I have never seen you before."

Andrea pressed her hand so forcibly that the young uttered a slight cry.

"I am your brother, Madame!" he said, in a deep, constrained voice.

"My brother!" cried Lucrezia, stupefied.

"Silence!" said Andrea. "Are your servants faithful to you?"

"They were placed here by the Count."

"Silence, then! For I have many things to say to you, Lucrezia, which your ears alone may hear. Is there any place here where we may be secure from the observation of spies?"

Lucrezia rose.

"Come," said she.

Then she took Andrea's hand, and with her other band, as white and beautifully modeled as those of the women of Albania, she pushed aside the rich draperies which covered the door. Then she drew him rapidly through a long suite of apartments.

At every step there was evidence that the most sumptuous wealth, and all the resources of Italian art, had been devoted to the adornment of the dwelling.

The countenance of Andrea Vitelli had now lost its ordinarily carefree expression, and as the wealth and the gallery of masterpieces and precious objects which surrounded Lucrezia Mammone became apparent, his forehead became proportionately clouded.

At length, Lucrezia opened a glass door, leading to a flight of marble steps, that gave access to the garden, which was laid out in a manner both simple and graceful. Its chief characteristic was a quantity of large trees surrounding a piece of turf through which ran a branch of the Nera.

Still leading him the hand, Lucrezia said, at length, pointing to a bank of turf:

"Sit down; no one but I will be able to hear you here."

Andrea sat down, and, for an instant, remained silent; then, whilst he was still wrapped in a reverie, Lucrezia passed her arm gently round his neck.

"My brother," she murmured, "how much I shall love you!"

Andrea, trembling, coldly repulsed her embrace, whilst he replied:

"I have always loved you, my sister."

"But why, then, repulse me?"

"I have many things to say to you," replied Vitelli in a deep, sad voice.

"My God! My God!" murmured the poor young girl. "I feel in the depths of my heart deep pleasure and deep pain! It is as though a great happiness and a great misery are struggling for the possession of me."

"You are right, Lucrezia," replied Andrea, gravely. "A great happiness and a great misery do await you. Listen to me. After fifteen years of exile, during which I have thought of you every day, and every day offered up my prayers for you, I have returned, strong and powerful, to this town from which I was driven, poor and helpless. I did not know whether you were dead or alive. But it was necessary that I should know; for in the whole world, with the exception of my son, who is an infant, I have nothing but you to love."

"Ah!" cried the young woman, while a strange gleam of joy lit up her countenance, "you have a son?"

"Listen to me, Madame!" interrupted the stranger. "I am Andrea Vitelli, Prince of Monteleone, Sovereign Seigneur of Ascoli; and you are the Countess Lucrezia Vitelli."

"Is it possible?"

"And it is said that Lucrezia Mammone has lost her good her name."

The poor woman, thus addressed, burst into a passion of sibs.

"Is it true, sister?" demanded Andrea.

Lucrezia hesitated for a moment, then, bowing her head low, she replied:

"It is true."

"Lucrezia Mammone is spoken of," rejoined Andrea, sadly, "in all the towns of Italy. Her beauty and her unrivaled charm of person and mind are mentioned everywhere. Yes, sister; she is spoken of in a manner which does sully the name of our father from Naples to Venice!"

Lucrezia's head was buried between her hands.

"The name of our father," she murmured, "the name of Vitelli—a name more noble than the name of any king! Oh, you are right, my brother! I have upon me now a great happiness and a great misery!"

"This morning," continued Andrea, "when I arrived in Spoleto, where I expected to find you, you were the first person whom I happened to see. You were being carried on a litter through the main boulevard. I followed you because you were beautiful, and because the loneliness of my life has given me the habit of plunging into foolish adventures. I did not know name. This evening, I returned to the front of your house, and found three gallants under your windows."

Lucrezia drew herself up, and, while a gleam of pride illumined her countenance, replied:

"Boasters and liars who are but too happy if they can pretend to have received a smile!"

"They laughed as they uttered your name," said Andrea, "and I drew my sword upon them."

"Oh! My brother! My brother!"

"While I was fighting, a man came out of your house."

"Yes! A man with a noble heart," cried Lucrezia, as she lowered her eyes. "A man who respects me, and whom I love. But how did you find out that Lucrezia Mammone was your sister?"

"In the palace of Count Ercole, there is a woman who was formerly in the service of our mother—Mercedes."

"Mercedes," repeated Lucrezia.

"I have questioned her. She told me everything. And now, Lucrezia, it is necessary that you should know the history of our family."

"I know it, brother! Ercole and Francis Vitelli were cousins. The old Prince of Monteleone was equally attached to them; but Francis died young, and Count Ercole inherited immense possessions."

"Francis died young because he was murdered," interrupted Andrea.

"Our father?" said Lucrezia, with a trembling voice.

"Yes, our father. Those who said that the old Prince of Monteleone was equally affectionate towards the two cousins lied. You were too young to understand it then, Lucrezia, but I remember it clearly. Listen!

"After the death of our good and virtuous mother, Countessa Pia Vitelli, the Prince of Monteleone sent for my father to inform him that he meant to make him his heir.

"The Prince resided in Spoleto, and dwelt in the palace where Count Ercole Vitelli now lives.

"We all came here—my father, you and I, and a poor relation whom my father supported out of charity.

"That poor relation is today Count Ercole, Prince of Monteleone, and Sovereign Seigneur of Ascoli."

"Count Ercole!" exclaimed Lucrezia.

"Yes; he! Mercedes also accompanied us."

"Mercedes has never mentioned that to me," said the young woman.

"Mercedes had reasons for concealing many things, from you, my sister; but be patient, and you shall know all.

"When we arrived here in Spoleto, the Prince gave us a magnificent reception, and, for my father's sake, was very gracious to our poor relation Ercole, who was quiet, complaisant, clever, and useful, and was the most devoted cousin there could possibly be."

Andrea pronounced these last words bitterly.

"We were living tranquilly in Spoleto, when our father experienced the first symptoms of a strange malady, which seemed to eat away at his lungs and entrails. Ercole tended him with a devotedness that touched the hearts of all those who witnessed it. He spent whole nights by the bedside of he whom he called his benefactor. He would not permit any hired servant to perform the services which the sick man required. He prepared the medicines himself, and administered them with his own hand. It was only to the Signora Mercedes, who had now become the general superintendent of the household, that he would now and then transfer the performance of this duty.

"Nevertheless, our father grew weaker by the day; while the old Prince of Monteleone was himself advancing closer to the edge of the grave.

"As I have already said, Lucrezia, you were too young then to be able to form any conception of what was happening, but I observed and understood everything.

"It seemed as though some implacable genius had enveloped the House of Vitelli in the cloud of his evil influence. The servants, plunged into the depth of sadness, performed their duties in mournful silence. No one in all the palace spoke except under his breath. As for me, I wandered from room to room, seeking ever to approach my father, but was invariably stopped on the threshold, either by Ercole, who would coldly say to me: 'Go away, Andrea, it is dangerous for young persons to breathe the air of sickrooms,' or by Mercedes, who would say, 'Don't come in; you will disturb him; he's asleep.'

"So that, never seeing our father, I had no means of judging what turns his malady was taking.

"This went on for a long time, a very long time, until a certain night, when I was awakened by a great clamor. I slept in a chamber near to that in which our father lay sick. I was frightened; but we sleep heavily when we are young, and I was not certain whether I was dreaming or really awake.

"I arose, still half-asleep and half-awake, and the idea came into my head to raise a thick drapery which hung over a door which had been long unused.

"I put my eye to the keyhole.

"And then, my sister, I saw a terrible and heartrending sight."

As Andrea uttered these words, drops of sweat fell from his forehead.

Lucrezia trembled.

At length, Andrea continued:

"The chamber into which I looked was large, and feebly illuminated by a night lamp.

"In spite of the obscurity, however, I could see that for a long time no one had taken the trouble to clean it, and that it had an aspect of the most deplorable neglect. The furniture was scattered in disorder in all directions.

"In the middle of the room there was a low bed, the sheets and blankets of which hung onto the floor; and on that bed lay a man who made one melancholy to look at.

"It was our father!

"His hair and beard had grown very long during his illness. He was pale and thin to the most frightful extent. His large hollow eyes were fixed with an unchanging stare upon the ceiling; and I should have thought that he was dead, if I had not seen his breast rise and fall with the efforts of painful respiration.

"At the head of the bed was Ercole Vitelli; at the foot, Mercedes. Both were deadly pale, and calm to an

extent which seemed terrible to me. Their eyes were often fixed upon our father. From time to time, the former
put a cup to his lips, saying at the same time: 'Drink,
drink, cousin!'

"The sick man drank mechanically, and then said:
'Enough! Enough! It burns me!'

"Mercedes seemed to me to shiver as she heard his
voice, but Ercole smiled.

"Once I heard Mercedes speak, and she said: 'God
will not have pity on us on the day of judgment.'

"To which Ercole replied: 'God will do what he
chooses; and I shall do what I choose. I must be a Prince,
and this man must die!'

"Our father turned his lackluster eyes towards him
and said: 'Who speaks of death?'

"Neither of his companions answered but, looking
at each other, placed fingers on their lips.

"Suddenly the noise that I had heard was renewed,
to a greater extent than before, and many voices cried
out, loud enough for my father to hear:

" 'The old Prince of Monteleone is dead!'

"And as he heard them, to the infinite terror of
Mercedes and Ercole, our father suddenly raised himself
upright, and 'said:

" 'May God receive the soul of my noble relative
and friend, the Sovereign Prince of Monteleone! Cousin
Ercole, be so good as to give me my velvet doublet. Although I do not feel well, it is necessary that I should
mount my horse, and go to receive the investiture of the
principality; for I have a son, Cousin Ercole!'

"He arose, pale and wan as a specter; and then the
two criminals, seized with affright, were on the point of
taking flight, when Mercedes, finding courage in the

45

very excess of her peril, locked the door and said to Ercole:

" 'We must finish it at once!'

" 'My doublet! My doublet! And my sword!' cried our father.

"And then, as he was advancing towards the door, Ercole closed his fist and gave him a blow to the stomach, which knocked him back upon the couch. The blow had a sad, sad sound, and our poor father fell back, crying out, with a deep, hollow voice:

" 'Traitor!'

"I also wished to cry out; but from the moment I had begun to witness the scene, it seemed as though a leaden bond had been placed upon my mouth.

"Mercedes, at the sound of her master's voice, sank down on her knees.

"It was Ercole who repeated: '*We must finish it at once!*'

"He went to the back of the bed, seized a pillow and pressed it violently on the face of the sick man. I saw the limbs of the victim struggle convulsively for few moments, and then fall, inert.

"For about ten minutes there was complete silence—a silence which seemed to me at the time to endure for an age. A passing thought flashed through my brain that, struck motionless by the Divine vengeance, Mercedes and Ercole were unable to move their homicidal arms.

"At length, however, the silence was broken. Mercedes took away the pillow, and ventured to look upon the face beneath it. Our father was dead!

" 'It is finished,' said Mercedes, 'and you are a Prince!'

"At that moment, the lamp died out and it seemed to me an omen that the hopes of the Vitelli were extinguished.

"The day now began to break, and by the doubtful light of dawn, I saw Ercole and Mercedes, like two demons, hovering about the corpse. They stretched it out upon the bed, and then, opening the chamber door, uttered cries and lamentations, which soon gathered around all the people of the house.

"As for myself, it all seemed to me like a dream. When I attempted to rise, I fell upon the floor."

At this point of the narrative Andrea paused, and Lucrezia raised her face, which, until now, she had held buried in her hands. The terrible story she had just heard had rendered her pale as death.

"That was not the last crime," she said, "committed by Count Ercole."

"I have not finished yet," replied Andrea, and he continued his tale with a firm voice.

"When I recovered consciousness, I found myself in a neighboring castle of the Apennines. You were with me, my sister; and I remember that the first time I found myself alone with you in the garden, I pressed you in my arms, and bathed you with my tears.

"On the following day, as though the matter had been arranged between Ercole and the bandits of the Abruzzi, a hundred brigands attacked the castle.

"They did not kill anyone, but took me prisoner.

"For performing this service, Ercole paid them a liberal sum.

"I was twelve years of age, and I might soon become dangerous.

"My new masters and I reached the mountains in two hours, and when we had arrived amongst them, my captors began to converse amongst themselves in low tones.

" 'Besides,' I heard the chief say, 'it would be a pity to take away the life of such a child; he is robust and well made; let us keep him with us; he will make a pleasant companion.'

"I understood from this that I had run a narrow risk of suffering my father's fate; and thanked God for preserving my life, that I might punish his assassin.

"I was carried to the bandits' camp, and lived amongst them.

"I grew up the companion of these men; became pert in the use of arms, and intrepid in the midst of danger.

"I always said to myself: *When I shall have a hundred armed men under my command, I will return to Spoleto and protect my sister.*

"For this idea had possession of my mind before even that of vengeance.

"And now—this very hour—I have a thousand swords at my command! For I am Demonio, the Chief of the Mountain."

"Demonio!" exclaimed Lucrezia. "The brave, the strong, the fearsome?"

Andrea gestured proudly as he replied:

"They have deprived me of all that my birth had endowed me; but I have acquired a power greater than that which should have devolved upon my father. Ten provinces tremble at the name of Demonio.

"But why speak of that that?" he murmured. "It is of you that I wish to speak, my sister. I have just returned from Calabria. I have placed my men in the pay and under the protection of Spain, that I might come to you—that I might be at hand to protect you. And now, my sister, as I find that you are past protection, tell me how I may avenge you!"

"You shall hear me and you shall judge me," replied Lucrezia. "You yourself shall decide whether I ought to live or die."

As she uttered these words, her beautiful head was inspired with an entirely new expression. She was no longer a girl, careless as one of Moschus's nymphs,[8] but a young woman, the serious lines of whose face belonged more to the austere type of Christian art. Lucrezia was not false to her blood; a word, a name, had inspired her with her natural pride.

Andrea gazed at her moment with passionate tenderness.

The scene was one of serious grandeur. The old *régime*, the fundamental idea of that old and beautiful world, which day by day fades from before our eyes, was present in this scene in all its completeness.

The brother was sufficient judge for his sister, and the sister ready for the sacrifice, as the Iphigenia of the past,[9] obedient to the Fates, was ready to seal with her

---

[8] Moschus, ancient Greek bucolic poet born in Syracuse who flourished around 150 BC. His few surviving works consist of an epyllion, the *Europa*, three bucolic fragments and a short bucolic poem *Runaway Love*, and an epigram in elegiac couplets. His surviving bucolic material is short on pastoral themes and is largely erotic and mythological.

[9] Iphigenia, daughter of King Agamemnon and Queen Clytemnestra a Princess of Argos. Agamemnon offended the goddess Artemis, who retaliated by commanding him to kill Iphigenia as a sacrifice so his ships could sail to Troy. In some versions, Iphigenia is sacrificed at Aulis, but in others, Artemis rescues her. In that version, she goes to the Taurians and meets her brother Orestes.

blood the grand principle *Noblesse Oblige*—that device which envelopes dead chivalry as a flag of honor.

Nature herself seemed to have taken pains to create a fitting framework to the scene. The moon, which had just risen above the horizon, silvered the crests of the lofty trees, whose majestic shadows stretched across the broad turf, and far up the walls of the palace. At the end of the garden, the waters of the Nera, sparkling with a thousand brilliant points like stars, flowed calm and silent between the thickets on its banks. In the distance, through the trees, could be seen a portion of the Vitelli palace, the windows of which now began to be illumined, one after the other. The hour for the *fête* to commence was at hand.

Lucrezia resumed the conversation, and said:

"The story of my life is a sad one, brother; it is only right that you should know the truth; so listen in your turn, and judge me!

"The farthest back that I can remember is when I was in that castle, at the foot of the Apennines, of which you just now spoke.

"The woman who waited on me was that Mercedes whose crime... But at that time, I believed that she loved me, and I loved her.

"I was happy all day long; I ran about the beautiful park, and, in the evening, I listened with delight to the marvelous legends of the mountain.

"The first time that I saw Count Ercole, I was fourteen years of age. He thought that I was beautiful, and from that moment, my whole life was changed.

"Musicians were brought to the castle. I was induced to dance and sing. I was clothed in rich dresses; and the diamonds I was presented with were worthy of a Princess.

"I was young and foolish, and all this filled me with de-light.

" One day, Count Ercole came to the castle with a priest, and asked me if I would be his wife."

Andrea made a gesture of surprise.

Lucrezia continued:

"My first inclination was to refuse; for I had already seen Angelo hunting amidst the mountains; but Mercedes in whom I had confidence, said to me: '*It must be.*'

"So I consented.

"The ceremony took place, and the Count gave me his ring at God's holy altar."

"But," exclaimed Andrea, who during the last few moments had scarcely been able to repress his impatience, "Ercole was married."

"I have learned that since, brother," replied Lucrezia. "I have learned that what was then done was an infamous insult to the majesty of Heaven, and the trustfulness of a poor young girl. For a month, I believed that I was Count Ercole's wife, but at the end of that time, I found that he had another Countess Vitelli in Spoleto, a wife whose rights were recognized by all the world, whilst mine were buried in the distant obscurity of the old castle of the Abruzzi.

"To learn this was a terrible blow—but only to my pride, for I still thought of myself as the daughter of a humble farmer from the valleys.

"I had never loved him whom I called my husband, and when I discovered his abominable treason, I detested him.

"He had only twice crossed the threshold of my bed chamber.

"But the third time…"

Lucrezia suddenly checked herself, and for a moment paused.

"Brother," she at length continued, "I conceal from you nothing. It is you who will have to decide whether I shall live or die. I am prepared for anything, and shall not appeal your sentence.

"Alas! I avenged myself, as fools are apt to do, upon myself. One evening, the Count found in front of the door of my bedchamber the sword of one of the Condottieri of the mountain.

"I had resolved to return insult for insult by taking a lover; and the stroke I had aimed at the Count wounded him deeply; for, after a fashion, he loved me.

"I had become the mistress of a cavalier whom I had drawn to me in my anger; and a year later, I was the mother of a girl."

"Ah!" cried Andrea, who had hitherto listened, plunged in a gloomy reverie, "you have a daughter, then?"

"Yes, the child of a blind moment of fury and hazard, my brother," replied Lucrezia. "A poor angel, who would have been in this world my sole joy, my sole hope, if I had not thus met with you. But now, brother, my life no longer belongs to me. You will pronounce judgment upon me, and have pity upon my child.

"My child," she resumed, in passionate tones, "is so beautiful and good; and if you take pity upon her, for all that her poor mother has suffered, she will only have to offer up thanks at the throne of the great Almighty God!"

"And I," murmured Vitelli, as though he were speaking to himself, "have a son."

As Lucrezia heard these words, she clasped her hands, and, gazing on her brother with a look of supplication, exclaimed:

"Then my daughter will be happy!"

"Continue your story," said Andrea, in reply.

"Ercole Vitelli still loved me," she continued. "With a love which seemed to increase day by day and I, who believed that I was alone upon the face of the earth, I accepted the disgrace which even now has suffused my face with so much shame.

"I returned to Spoleto. It was absolutely necessary for me to numb my conscience in some way or other, and I plunged into a whirlpool of *fêtes* and pleasures. I passed as the Count's mistress; and I had so much influence over him, that my daughter was cradled in the palace side by side with the legitimate heiress of the real wife of Vitelli."

As she said this, she turned towards the palace, the illuminated front of which now shone through the boughs of the trees.

"See!" she cried, stretching out her arm. "See! Behind those lit windows, behind that one which is more dimly lit than the others, is the cradle of my daughter.

"I do not know whether I shall ever see her again, brother, for I am ready. Yes! When I shall have finished what I have to say to you, you will have no need to condemn me. I shall understand your silence.

"During that year I have been at Spoleto—you will understand what I mean—no one has attracted my attention.

"Up to this hour, I must acknowledge, I have done nothing to quench the calumny. The Count's love my power and his jealousy augmented it."

"Ah!" said Andrea knitting his brow. "I am your judge, Madame. Defend yourself better than that."

Lucrezia gazed upon him with a confident glance.

"Defend myself?" she exclaimed, with bitter smile. "Do I not know that I am utterly lost? I am the queen of the freest ballrooms, of the merriest festivals; as you said just now, my name is mentioned in terms of dishonor in every town in Italy. *I am Lucrezia Mammone*, and to-morrow, if I should live so long, I should wish to be Lucrezia Vitelli. Do you hear me, brother?"

Andrea listened to this in silence.

"Must I die, then?" asked the young girl, in a voice low but firm.

To this, Andrea, as pale as death, replied, in broken words:

"My sister! My sister! Perhaps there is some remote corner of Italy…"

"What?" interrupted Lucrezia. "You wish that I should hide myself! No! I will not hide myself. The question is, must I die?"

And then, as Andrea still remained silent, she pointed with a calm gesture towards the tiny lake, formed by the waters of the Nera in the midst of the lawn, and murmured:

"The water is deep."

The beams of the moon glimmered mysteriously through the foliage of the trees, and fell upon the tranquil pool.

"My brother," continued Lucrezia in calm, sad tones, which vibrated harmoniously through the silence, like a funeral chant, "I am proud; I cannot consent to put those whom I love to shame; the water is deep, and death is easy."

Andrea buried his forehead between his hands.

Lucrezia arose.

"One kiss, brother," she said. "The first and the last."

Andrea drew her towards him, and gave her a passionate embrace. She then took a step back.

"Look at me," she said, firmly. "Is it possible that I could live without dishonoring the name of Vitelli?"

Andrea's breast heaved with a deep sob, but he still kept silence.

With a gentle smile, Lucrezia glided, pale and spirit-like through the moonbeams to the edge of the little lake.

"My brother!" called the young woman, from afar, "be a father to my child, and avenge me. Adieu!"

Raising her arms towards Heaven, she stooped forward, while the name of Angelo hovered on her lips.

The moonbeams danced upon the agitated waters of the pool.

After a few moments, the water resumed its calm and silent course between the lonely banks.

But just then a boat, which had lain concealed under the shadow of some large willows, shot from the bank.

In the boat there was but one man, who rowed with all his force towards the pool.

The moon veiled itself behind a cloud, its last ray having gleamed upon the blond locks of the rower, the young Cavalier Angelo.

The rough bandit, Andrea Vitelli, whom both his friends and his enemies had united in naming *Demonio*, wept and prayed before the cross of his sword, planted in the earth.

At the end of some seconds, Andrea arose and plucked his sword from the ground.

He turned towards the palace of Count Ercole.

"There!" he murmured. "Her daughter is there! Her daughter is there! It is death, perhaps; but she has died well. She…"

His legs trembled under his body. He struggled against his anguish, supported by that wild pride of the gentleman, which, like the ancient stoicism, could not be influenced by the affections, and knew how to yield only to the power of death.

Andrea traversed the garden and the shrubberies with tottering steps; but as he went on, his strength returned to him.

After a few moments, he found himself in front of the Vitelli palace.

The area appeared deserted.

He searched for that window more dimly lit than the others, which his sister had pointed out to him from the garden.

When he had found it, he fixed his dagger between two stones, and, with his sword between his teeth, began to climb the lofty well.

In the meantime, moving figures became visible from behind the corners of the neighboring houses; and the street, which had until now been completely deserted, became filled with persons, who advanced with stealthy steps.

At the moment when Andrea had reached the balcony, one of the mysterious persons raised his broad-brimmed hat, and displayed the sinister countenance of Capitan, Count Ercole's confidential agent.

He turned towards his companions, and, making a mute sign of intelligence, said:

"It is not often that one climbs high for the purpose of throwing one's self into the clutches of the wolf."

IV. The Two Children.

It was a chamber, lit only by the dim and oscillating light of a night lamp.

Two cradles, surrounded by silk hangings, were side by side.

Vast curtains draped their ample folds in front of a lofty window, the embrasure of which was large enough to serve for an alcove.

Beside the two children, Mercedes, the duenna, murmured the conclusion of her Pater Nosters.

The light of the lamp fell full upon the countenance of the two children, and seemed to form around them a gentle aureole. They were little girls, and were charming in their smiling sleep.

Mercedes suddenly interrupted herself in the utterance of her prayers, and exclaimed with a trembling voice:

"Ah! I thought that I heard something…"

She checked herself for a moment, and made the sign of the cross.

"Ah! Poor wretched woman that I am!" she continued. "I am always, always in a state of terror; my memories terrify me; and my sleep is full of dreadful dreams."

She looked at the clock which hung on the wall.

"Nine o'clock," she murmured. "How long shall I have to wait for the breaking of the day? My God, will he return? Must I once more gaze on that pale face which is so like the face of the dead? Of Andrea! Andrea! Francis Vitelli, Prince of Monteleone!"

She shivered from head to foot.

"How long he suffered!" she continued. "How large and hollow were his eyes! How changed was his voice, when he said to us: 'Give me my doublet; I will mount my horse.' A dead mounting a horse!" she added, with a hysterical laugh.

Then she proceeded in a softer tone:

"...And he—Andrea—the young man—all the past seemed to suddenly become the present to me at the sight of him! The chamber, the bed, the ghostly-looking old man, and—the pillow! Oh, the pillow!"

She buried her face in her hands.

The two children smiled and slept.

A sound came from the direction of the window.

The duenna trembled a second time, more violently than at first.

"This time," she murmured, "I cannot have been deceived. I heard..."

Then, recovering herself, and endeavoring to smile, she said:

"How foolish I am! It was the wind. What can I have to fear in a palace like this, so well guarded, and lit up for a *fête*!"

As she uttered these words, one of the panes of the window, broken by sudden blow, fell in with a crash, and the sound of a spurred boot was heard upon the chamber floor.

The duenna jumped up, startled.

The draperies, which concealed the embrasure, glided back upon their cornice pole, and the figure of Andrea appeared between their silken folds.

The duenna uttered one cry, and then fell as if she had been struck dead.

Andrea paid no attention to the woman's terror, but advanced straight towards the cradle.

58

But as he stretched out his hand. He paused and turned pale.

He had come to find one infant, and there were two.

Which of them was his sister's daughter?

He gazed now at the one, now at the other. Each of them was equally beautiful in their calm and smiling slumber.

He shook the duenna to arouse her, that he might interrogate her; but she remained motionless.

"Which can it be?" he murmured. "Which?"

And he stood in a state of indecision in front of the double cradle.

Once more he roughly shook Mercedes; but she gave no signs of life.

"Ah, well!" he murmured. "As this is the case, I must take them both."

As he said this, he lifted the two children and wrapped hem gently in the folds of his cloak.

Then he proceeded towards the balcony, with the intention of departing as he had come.

But when he had once more pushed aside the heavy drapery, he saw that the balcony was now filled with armed men.

He drew his sword, and rushed towards the door.

As the door opened, it disclosed another band of armed men with drawn swords—Capitan, as becomes a brave chief, standing behind them.

Then the voice of Count Ercole made itself heard:

"Seize him!" he cried. "Seize him, dead or alive."

"Kill him! Kill him!" cried Capitan, more frank than his master.

Andrea placed himself with his back against the wall. At first, he made as though he were about to defend himself; but suddenly, as if a happy idea had occurred to him, he uncovered the faces of the two children and, raising his sword above their heads, exclaimed:

"Ercole Vitelli, stand back, you and your men, or you will be without a daughter!"

This threat fell like a thunderbolt upon the heart of the old Count, and made him tremble violently.

"My daughter!" he cried, in a stifled voice. "Fall back! Fall back! Let him pass!"

He was pale, and his locks fell over his damp forehead.

Capitan's men drew to one side, and Andrea passed, his head erect.

Before crossing the threshold of the palace, he turned and said:

"Ercole Vitelli, my sister is dead. One day, we shall meet again!"

He gained the street, and speedily reached the spot where he had left his horse, fastened to the iron ring in the wall. The horse neighed with impatience. Andrea loosened him, leaped into the saddle with his double burden, and set forth at a gallop from Spoleto on the road leading to the mountains.

PART ONE

I. The Woman in Grey

The bandits of the Abruzzi were not, properly speaking, mere highway robbers; for, as we have already said, these lawless men played a part in the political disturbances in Italy, and lived in the pay of any party which would employ them. When the struggle ended, they retreated to their mountains, where they had constructed formidable fortresses.

It is to one of these inaccessible forts, built like the nests of birds of prey, on the highest crests of the mountains, that we will now take our readers.

Fifteen years have elapsed since the day when Andrea Vitelli set out from Spoleto, carrying with him Count Ercole's two children.

Since that time, Andrea had had many conflicts with the troops of Austria and Spain; passed his life in wandering amongst the mountains; and undergone all the various chances of war.

His renown had increased, and three thousand men now obeyed his orders.

It was the year 1665, shortly after the death of Massaniello.[10] Italy was in that state of agitated quiet which ordinarily succeeds repressed revolutions. The

---

[10] Massaniello (an abbreviation of Tommaso Aniello) (1622-1647), Italian fisherman who became leader of the revolt against the rule of Habsburg Spain in Naples in 1647.

regular troops had been withdrawn to their barracks. The Free Companies had plunged once more into the recesses of the mountains.

The small army of bandits and soldiers of fortune, which obeyed Andrea Vitelli's command, had pitched its tents in that portion of the Apennines which is nearest to Spoleto, on a plateau a quarter of a league in circumference, on the top of a mountain which was somewhat lofty, but had a gentle slope.

The sides of the mountain were covered with forests, and seamed with the beds of torrents and deep but narrow openings, which were small valleys, in which were found the warm air and the soft vegetation of the plains.

In the middle of the plateau rose a fortress that had recently been built by order of Andrea Vitelli. It was sufficiently spacious to contain a considerable garrison, and its ramparts which were of a thickness of which modern structures afford no example, could with impunity defy the imperfect artillery of the period.

From the summit of these inaccessible ramparts, the eye embraced an immense extent of country; below, it plunged into the immense depths which surrounded the mountain. Looking upwards, it could traverse the blue crests of the mountain-chain, which stood against the sky, like the marshaled tents of a camp of giants.

It was here that Andrea had planted his flag, and laid his hearth-stone.

A large detachment always occupied the fort, and served as its garrison. The remainder of the army, and especially those who acted as shepherds and hunters, had erected their tents and their cottages around the fortress upon the plateau, and thus presented to the eye of the observer the primitive organization of feudal society.

Most of the men had women and children with them, which gave to this camp of bandits the aspect of a populous, lively village, filled with both happiness and plenty.

Those who dwelt in it seemed to vie with each other as to who should sing the most heartily whilst furbishing arms, or engaging in the various domestic occupations. Men, women, and children wore garments of brilliant colors, in harmony with the feelings of their possessors.

The camp bustled with incessant activity. There was a continuous coming and going. Here, a party was setting out on an expedition; there, another party was returning from one. On this side appeared an animated group, preparing for the chase, and on that side could be seen a cluster of those who were on the point of starting to gather in their own cattle, together, perhaps, with those belonging to others.

Here and there burned huge fires of fir, and above the glowing embers roasted game, or huge quarters of beef.

On the roads which wound along the mountain sides might be seen, in various directions, small parties of men with muskets on their shoulders.

Lower down, on the slopes of the mountain, were visible herds of cattle and flocks of sheep and goats, tended by some bandit, who stood motionless, wrapped in his cloak, and resting on his musket.

The sun had risen an hour since, and gave the promise of a magnificent day. The mountain breeze had not as yet chased away the grey mist which slept in the depths of the gorges, and blotted the lower levels of the country from the sight. It was a charming morning.

The sentinels on the battlemented ramparts of the fortress seemed themselves to be in a dreamy contemplation of those magnificent mountains, which Salvator re-produced so grandly in his dramatic landscapes.[11]

Suddenly the sound of a horse's hooves was heard on the planks of the drawbridge, and a young girl came out of the fortress at gallop. She was about seventeen years-old.

She was a beautiful creature, proud in her bearing and bold in her movements.

Her regular and charming features bore an expression which was at once resolute and piquant. She managed her black mountain steed with all the skill of an accomplished cavalier.

Her dress was in harmony with the expression of her countenance. On her black and waving locks, which resembled those of the women in Titian's pictures,[12] was small grey felt hat, adorned with a simple heron's plume.

A black velvet jacket, ornamented with silver buttons, enclosed her symmetrical bust.

At her waist she wore a pretty dagger, with a bronze handle, and a pair of pistols, inlaid with silver, which were very jewels of arms.

---

[11] Salvator Rosa (1615-1673), an Italian Baroque painter, poet, and printmaker, who was active in Naples, Rome, and Florence. As a painter, he is best known as "unorthodox and extravagant," as well as being a "perpetual rebel" and a proto-Romantic.

[12] Tiziano Vecelli (or Vecellio) (c.1488/1490-1576), an Italian painter, the most important member of the 16th-century Venetian school. Recognized by his contemporaries as "The Sun Amidst Small Stars," he was equally adept with portraits, landscapes, mythological and religious subjects. His painting methods, particularly in the application and use of color, exercised a profound influence not only on painters of the Italian Renaissance, but on future generations of Western art.

The young amazon traversed the camp at a gallop; and, as she passed amongst them, men, women, and children interrupted their labors or their sports for the purpose of giving her a gracious salute.

"The Lady!" they cried on every side. "The Lady Regina!"

Everyone gazed after her, as she bounded along on her horse, with pleasure and interest.

As for Regina, she responded gaily to the salutations addressed to her, seemed even desirous of calling them forth, and frankly displayed the pleasure she experienced at exciting so much admiration.

Regina soon disappeared along a deep road which led from the plateau, and wound like a snake down the steep sides of the mountain. For a few moments, the iron hooves of the horse could be heard dashing against the flint of the road; but gradually the sound grew faint, and faded away like a dream.

A quarter of an hour afterwards, a second young girl came from the fortress. Although there was some likeness between her and the first, there was also much dissimilarity. There was a resemblance between the features, but a great difference in the expression.

Both were brunettes; both were somewhat under seventeen years of age; and the figures of both had those fine and supple outlines which are so agreeable to a poetic imagination.

But, while the bearing and expression of the first denoted a character that was bold, impetuous, proud, and resolute, the second showed by her timid steps and gestures that her nature was made up of goodness of heart and feminine grace.

Her name was Alma.

She had neither the prancing steed nor the brilliant costume of Regina, but walked along slowly, simply clothed in a robe that fastened round her waist by a pale blue ribbon.

Around her, as she proceeded, pressed at every step women, children, and old men. It need scarcely be said, however, that the latter were not numerous, since it was seldom that the people of the mountain did not meet with their death before having reached the later period of life.

Alma responded to the salutes and good wishes of all with infinite gentleness. She asked after the health of all; succored those were sick and consoled the afflicted. At every step of her road, the damascened clasps of the pretty alms-purse, which hung from her waist, were opened. No hand that was stretched out towards her for charity was withdrawn empty.

On those who asked nothing, she bestowed her exquisite smile, radiant and pure, as that of a Madonna.

"Well, what news?" she said, as she passed along.

"Ah, Signora," replied one, giving the chief news of the day. "We live in strange times! There have been castles burned this night in the country around Spoleto, and the people of the mountain have had nothing to do with it."

"But does no one know?"

Old men, women, and children shook their heads with an air of mystery, and for sole reply pronounced one name:

"Bel Demonio!"

But who was meant by that strange name?

Andrea Vitelli, also known to his men as Andrea Balbi, had formerly borne the *nom de guerre* of "Demonio," but it was not to him that that allusion was now made.

66

Bel Demonio was a fantastic hero of the mountain legends, whom it was impossible to describe or define.

According to all accounts, it was a being who was bold, cruel, and powerful; but while some declared that the creature was fair and beautiful as a girl, others were equally certain that he was as dark as Satan.

He made his expeditions at night, at the head of a dozen African Saracens, black as ebony, and wrapped up in great white shawls.

His castle was no one knew where, perhaps only known to the Devil himself.

Alma passed on her way.

When she had reached the extremity of the camp, she took the road by which Regina had disappeared an hour before.

She followed for some time the road usually traversed by men, horses, and cattle; but when she had descended two- thirds of the mountain's height, she went left along a sort of natural path, covered with grass, and descended into one of those hollows in the mountain sides which form, as it were, aerial valleys, and give to certain mountains of the Apennines so picturesque a character.

Alma descended into this verdant retreat, protected by elegant shrubs, and in which the air was at once fresh and warm.

The young girl paused at a spot where some rocks, covered with moss, formed an irregular mound. From this mass of rock, piled one upon the other, in picturesque pell-mell which would fill an artist with admiration, sprung a sparkling streamlet.

The water had formed for itself a bed through the trees, the thickets, and the rocks, and threw itself in cascades of white foam towards the lower part of the mountain.

Beside this spring was a stone, which was naturally formed into a shape which rendered it very serviceable as a seat. Alma sat down upon it and gazed for a moment upon the smiling prospect before her; then, after having plucked some flowers, she drew from her bosom a piece of embroidery, of which her fingers had woven the partly completed web of silk and gold.

Before recommencing her work, she looked around her with an air of mystery.

The embroidery already displayed three letters upon a scarlet velvet ground. An M, an A, and an R—MAR.

She had scarcely made the first movement with her needle when the approaching sounds of a horse's hooves made her raise her head and replace the embroidery in her bosom.

She saw Regina entering the valley, making her plunge and rear upon the turf, in a manner which seemed to threaten to unseat her.

Regina leaped lightly from her saddle, left the steed to pasture amongst the rocks, and ran to embrace Alma.

"Ah! What a beautiful bouquet!" she exclaimed, looking at the flowers which the latter bad gathered.

"I have gathered it for you," replied Alma.

Regina took the bouquet with pleasure, but at the end of a few minutes, she begun to pull it to pieces. She plucked from it one flower after another, and threw them into the spring to see them float along its current. Then she placed one in her hat, another in her bosom, and another in her horse's mane, and gave him the rest to eat.

"My poor bouquet!" cried Alma.

"Ah! Good Heavens! You are right!" exclaimed Regina.

They then both began to laugh aloud; but in her secret heart, Alma had a vague feeling of pain.

Perhaps it was not for Regina she had gathered the poor pretty flowers.

"You have not met with Mario, have you?" asked the amazon, with feigned indifference.

"No," replied Alma. "He was not at the fort when I left."

"And yet I told him yesterday evening that I should certainly take a ride on my horse on the mountain!"

Alma blushed, as she answered:

"You must not be angry with him; Uncle Andrea has doubtless sent him to relieve the sentinels."

"Well, well!" murmured the amazon. "You always excuse him."

Alma blushed still more; then she said, as though to change the subject of conversation:

"Have you heard the news?"

"What news?" demanded Regina.

"Bel Demonio descended last night into the plain…"

"Ah?"

"…And from top of the towers of the fort, two castles have been seen in smoking ruins."

"Ah?" again exclaimed the amazon, while a vivid scarlet colored her cheek.

"Who, then, is this Bel Demonio?" asked Alma in a low voice.

"Mario, perhaps," replied Regina, as she turned her head, with a smile.

"Mario?" replied Alma, energetically. "Mario? It is impossible, sister. Mario is brave, but he is generous and good."

The amazon bit her lip, as she answered:

"This Bel Demonio makes war, that is all! A soldier is naturally not as tender as a little girl. But it is idle to reason on such a fable. Bel Demonio is a myth, a dream, a phantom.."

"Everyone speaks about him."

"Everyone?" said Regina, with a mocking accent. "Yes! Everyone has seen him traversing the mountain-path at a gallop with his twelve Saracens, clothed in white—everyone! He glides like cloud across the pale beams of the moon. Everyone, forsooth! But who has seen him by the light of the sun? Listen, Alma," continued the amazon, as she seated herself on the stone beside her companion, "I am ready to wager that Bel Demonio is not as bad as people make him out. Whenever a castle is burned, whenever a ransom is extorted from a villa, it is Bel Demonio! Always Bel Demonio! My own opinion is that all the vagabonds of the Upper Abruzzi pay him the homage of attributing to him all their misdeeds."

"May God have pity on his soul! " exclaimed Alma.

"My poor dear sister!" pursued the amazon, in a voice in which there was a tone of pity and protection, "you are seventeen years-old, as am I, and you have hitherto occupied your time with nothing but children's tales. But there are other subjects which occupy the time of young girls—the young girls of the cities of Naples, of Florence, and even of Spoleto. Ah! If you only knew how many beautiful *fêtes* there are! If you could know how the music intoxicates, how the lights dazzle!"

"One would almost think that you had witnessed them yourself," interposed Alma, smiling.

It was now the turn of the amazon to blush.

"I?" she cried. "Alas! I am as you are, only a poor little savage, who has seen nothing at all; but I have listened to those them, and I dream…"

"Ah! You dream?"

"Yes! And my dreams are delicious! When I gallop along, alone, on my African steed, I imagine that I am really taking part in the scenes that have been described to me! I set out at night, jeweled and brilliant. Spoleto opens to me its gates; I enter the Palace of Santa Fiore or Vitelli, and then, ah! what a blaze there is of lights and diamonds! And oh! what beautiful flowers, and such charming, charming women! And then, my sister, my sister! how well the cavaliers look in their velvet and their lace! The handsomest, the most noble looking of the whole company, comes to me and asks me for a minuet. I lower my eyes, I blush—the blush of pleasure, my sister!—and then, then, I dance! I dance! And everywhere I go, I hear the voices of the women, who are jealous of me, and the voices of the men, who enthusiastically exclaim, 'She is beautiful! She is beautiful! She is beautiful!'"

Alma gave her companion a meaningful and significant look.

" 'She is beautiful!' repeated Regina, who became more and more animated as she spoke, and whose great black eyes burned with an ever-increasing fire. "And I glide into the warm atmosphere, fragrant with perfumes... I smile... I am happy... I am intoxicated, for I am the queen of the ball! It is as if incense were burning before me, and I hear voices continually repenting, 'She is beautiful! She is beautiful! She is beautiful!'"

"Well, my sister," said Alma, "that at least is true; for you are beautiful!"

"And then," continued Regina, who allowed herself to be carried away by her thoughts as though she were in a dream, "there are some who admire me; and after having allowed them to admire me for an instant, I vanish as though I were a vision. My horse awaits me at the city gate. I put him to the gallop! The gallop ! The cold air of the mountain paths is refreshing after the tepid air of the festal halls. The cold air of night touches my forehead as though it were a mysterious hand. I gallop! I gallop! But am I alone? What is that sound? A young gentleman comes up with me; he young and handsome, with a face proud and pale as that of Mario. He takes my hand... He loves me!"

Alma burst into a loud laugh.

"What?" she said. "Your dreams have lasted so long as all that, my sister?"

At these words, Regina appeared for a moment as one who has suddenly awakened.

She seemed for a time as though she wished to answer, but her mouth remained open, and her eyes remained fixed in a stare upon a woman who stood at some two hundred steps from the two girls, upon a projecting rock.

This woman, on her part, seemed to gaze upon the two young girls with the utmost curiosity.

She was tall, but her head inclined towards one shoulder with an air of fatigue; long dark locks, among which were visible some threads of silver, fell around her haggard cheeks ; while her eyes were large and hollow.

The appearance of this woman seemed to produce upon Regina a most painful impression. Alma had not seen her.

In the meantime, the stranger did not stir. She was clothed in a manner which was as strange as her whole appearance. Over her grey dress she wore a mantle, of which inclement weather had completely effaced the colors. Her hat had been similarly affected; and the whole effect of her costume was that, standing as she did, immoveable upon a projecting piece of the rocks, she seemed to mingle and be lost amidst their grey shadows.

The woman was still handsome, in spite of the ravages which time or poverty or some great grief had made upon her. At a distance, her wearied attitude gave her the appearance of being old; but, on looking at her nearer and more attentively, it could be readily perceived that she was not more than from thirty-five to thirty-six years-old. Her great black eyes, sunk deep into their orbits, were filed with an expression of the greatest sadness; and the same might be perceived in her mouth, and in all the lines of her countenance.

The strange woman gazed upon the two young girls. Her earnest eyes wandered from one to the other, and there was evident in all her bearing an expression of the deepest doubt; but every time that her eyes rested upon Regina, full of love, it seemed as though it were impossible for her to remove them. One might almost have imagined that the soul of the poor woman was about to quit its human framework, and blend itself for ever with that of the young girl.

Alma continued to smile; but Regina suddenly seized by the arm and pressed it forcibly, while she said in a whisper:

"*The Woman in grey!*"

It was easy to perceive, from the accent of her voice, that she was possessed for the moment with some superstitious terror. Alma turned her eyes towards the rock; but, far from being as terrified as her sister at the sight of the unknown woman, she only felt, when she perceived her, a generous, compassionate impulse.

"Are you frightened of that poor woman?" she asked of Regina.

"I am never frightened," replied Regina drily; and then, she suddenly added, in a tone which gave the lie to her words: "But—I don't know how it is—that strange creature comes so often across my path, that… that I am frightened of her."

"But see, Regina, with how much goodwill she seems to look at you."

"It is that appearance of goodwill which displeases me. This is not the first time that I have seen her. I have often met her far from here, and every time that I have seen her, her eyes have followed me with such a persistent gaze, that…"

Here, she interrupted herself for a moment, then continued, with a passionate gesture:

"Yes, yes; it is true, I am frightened of that woman!"

" She has suffered, suffered very much," said Alma. "It is easy that."

"Listen," replied Regina, in a whisper, "one of the men belonging to Andrea Vitelli's band, a native of Spoleto, told me that he recognized this woman. He assured me that he saw her some time ago, young, beautiful, and rich; but when I asked him how long ago this was, he could not tell. Perhaps she is a sorceress, who takes sometimes the form of a young girl, and sometimes that of an old woman…"

"Foolish girl!" replied Alma. "It is only some poor unhappy girl, reduced to living on alms."

"Well, it is possible," replied Regina, drily, "but see, she looks at us… She looks at us!"

"Why, what are you afraid of, Regina? You, so brave!"

The amazon suddenly arose.

"Come," she said.

"But," said Alma, who also rose, "we must not go without bestowing alms on that poor woman."

Regina looked at her companion with astonishment.

"What?" she said. "You would venture?"

Regina was as brave as a man in the presence of any physical danger, but she was utterly powerless before anything that seemed supernatural. With Alma. The contrary was the case; and at the sight of Regina's terror, she only began to smile.

"Oh," entreated the amazon, "pray do not go to her! Pray do not go to her! Some misfortune will happen to you!"

"If any misfortune happens to me," replied Alma, gently, "I shall not be so unjust as to attribute it to that poor woman."

And then, in spite of the prayers and remonstrances of Regina, Alma tranquilly walked towards the rock on which still stood, with an attitude of melancholy, the Woman in grey.

II. Mario Vitelli

Alma, to the great consternation of her companion, climbed the rock, and approached the Woman in grey, as this poor creature—who had been wandering about the tents of the Vitelli camp for the last two or three weeks—was already called.

She evidently watched the approach of the young girl with pleasure, and a strange smile lit up her countenance. Alma took a piece of silver from her alms-purse and presented it to her.

"Take it, poor woman," she said, with the light of benevolence on her brow.

The Woman in grey took the coin, but at the same time retained in her hand the hand of the young girl, and gazed on her long and fixedly, with an expression of love mingled with doubt and anxiety. Alma was at first a little frightened; but the gaze of the poor woman was so gentle that it reassured her, while at the same time it caused within her a strange emotion which astonished her.

The lips of the Woman in grey moved slowly, and Alma thought that she heard them pronounce words of which she could not understand the meaning:

"Which, my God! Which of the two?"

After some seconds, she raised Alma's hand to her lips, kissed it, and said:

"Thank you, my beautiful angel; I will keep this coin in remembrance of you."

Then she released the hand of the young girl, who ran off to rejoin her companion.

"What did she say?" cried Regina, when Alma had returned.

"She thanked me for what I gave her."

"But she took your hand, and I think she touched her lips with it."

"Yes, she kissed my hand out of goodness of heart."

Regina instinctively shrunk back, as she murmured:

"An evil spell is very quickly thrown! As for me, whether Mario does or does not come, I shall wait no longer. But see! She is still looking at me!"

"You may go, if you want," said Alma, "but I shall remain."

Regina turned upon her a quick and piercing glance.

"Ah!" she said. "You will remain!"

Then, after an instant during which she seemed wrapped in pensive thought, she murmured, as if some suspicion had then for the first time entered her heart:

"You will remain! Bah! It is impossible! But we will see, we will see!"

Then, suddenly turning towards her horse, she called out in a dry, clear voice:

"Fuoco!"

The little steed came neighing and trotting across the turf.

"Mount on the crupper!" then said Regina to her sister.

But Alma looked at her with a frightened gaze.

"Mount!" repeated the amazon, whose accent had become imperious, in spite of the smile which played on her lips.

"I do not dare," repeated Alma, who was really alarmed.

"When people are not afraid of sorceries, they can scarcely be afraid of riding a horse!" said the amazon, sarcastically.

And the same instant, she seized Alma in her arms, lifted her from the ground with a strength which no one could have suspected her to possess, and placed her upon the horse's crupper.

Alma trembled. Regina leaped into the saddle, and, striking her horse with her whip, set off at a gallop.

Alma, being unable to get off the horse, fastened her arms tightly round the waist of Regina, who burst into shouts of laughter, and urged her horse to its utmost speed.

"Oh, Nina! Nina!" said Alma, addressing her sister by her softest name. "Stop! Stop! I entreat you!"

"I intend to take you as far as the fort," replied Regina.

In the meantime, the Woman in grey, still standing on the projecting rock, watched this curious scene, which seemed very likely to end in some catastrophe. And as she watched it, she murmured, mechanically, as one is apt to murmur one of those refrains which haunt the memory:

"Which of the two? My God! Which of the two?"

When the horse had carried the two young girls away from track we have already mentioned, and they had left it for the beaten road which ascended the side of the mountain, the Woman in grey fell to her knees upon the rock and prayed.

In the meantime, the small steed, urged onwards by the whip of the amazon and the frightened cries of Alma, proceeded at its utmost speed; and when Regina at length wished to moderate it, she found that it was no longer obedient to her. It had taken the extreme border of the road, and galloped along it like a whirlwind.

Next to these two girls, at half a foot's distance, was the abyss. Regina grew pale; whilst Alma closed her eyes and recommended her soul to God.

Still the horse proceeded on its dangerous course.

At that moment, a tall young man, of some twenty years of age, appeared at an angle of the road. He was walking indolently, with a musket on his shoulder, and singing a mountain air.

As soon as he perceived the danger of the two young girls, he uttered a cry, and, throwing his musket to one side, placed himself on the extreme edge of the road to await the arrival of the horse.

When it came to where the young man was standing, the animal turned to one side, but not sufficiently quickly to prevent the former from seizing it with a firm hand by the bridle. It still ran some paces forward, forcing its captor to run with it, but soon stopped, vanquished by a strength greater than its own.

"Ah! Mario!" cried poor Alma. "You have saved our lives!"

He had not as yet looked at Regina.

Mario took Alma gently in his arms, and carried her to a bank, covered with turf, by the road side.

Regina watched this scene with a strange look. The tenderness of Mario for Alma displayed itself in his every gesture, in all the accents of his voice, in his features, and in his very attitude, and this, involuntarily, and even against his will.

It was evident that Regina was in pain.

"And how are you, Regina?" Mario said to her at length.

"I?" replied the amazon. Bitterly. "Are you about anxious about me, cousin Mario? For my part, I was not frightened, and I am sorry anyone should have taken the trouble to stop the horse!"

"What?" exclaimed the young man, astonished.

"Do you mean to say," cried Region, angrily, "that I am not capable of riding Fuoco along the edge of a torrent? You are very maladroit, cousin Mario Vitelli. The ridiculous cries of that little cousin of yours have made you fail in the respect which is due to me."

"Ah!" said Mario, saluting her.

Then, taking her hand, and kissing it, he added gaily:

"I hope, cousin, you will not challenge me! For in good sooth, you are a valiant little man rather than a girl!"

Although Mario uttered these words with the utmost cordiality, the amazon was piqued at them; and to conceal her anger, she spurred her horse, and used him as roughly as the most hardened horseman would have done, careless of the foam which whitened his bit, and of the sweat which streamed off his body.

In the meantime, Mario, having picked up his musket and thrown it over his left shoulder, had offered his right arm to Alma, who leaned upon it with an air of pleasure and affection.

Mario affected at first to make Regina a third in the conversation; but as she pouted and kept aloof, he at length left her to the society of Fuoco, who began to be in as bad a temper as her, and gave his whole attention to Alma. Regina followed them with a disturbed and thoughtful air.

We have omitted to say that Mario Vitelli was a handsome man of lofty stature, and a bust which was remarkable for its strength and elegance. He wore a little black mustache, partly turned up at the ends, as was the fashion of the times. His features were, at the same time, frank, joyous, and resolute. He generally walked with an indolent carelessness, and that lounging air peculiar to the young and the strong. But at the present moment, that vague spirit of negligence had disappeared from his manner completely, such power over him had the presence and the conversation of Alma.

Frequently, as they went along, Regina leaned gently forward, placing her head between the ears of Fuoco, and endeavored to hear some part of the intimate conversation which was being carried on between Mario and Alma; but the noise made by her horse's hooves on the hard road drowned it. Regina was pale, and her lips trembled.

A new circumstance now occurred to increase her sullen rage. During the conversation which she could not hear, there was a moment when the faces of Mario and Alma were turned towards each other. Their eyes met and rested on each other, as two friends who pass their arms round each other's necks, and rest against each other, shoulder to shoulder.

Regina, bent down upon her horse's mane, witnessed this clasping together of soul with soul; and she suddenly started up as if she had been bitten by a scorpion.

"Oh!" she exclaimed to herself. "They love each other! They love each other!" and the poor girl's heartfelt faint.

For that fanciful story she had told of what might occur when she departed from the *fêtes* of Spoleto—of that journey by night of two lovers in the mountain—ah! it was no mere dream!

Without saying a word, she gave her horse two or three strokes with her whip, with so heavy a hand that the wearied animal bounded forward, and although the road lay uphill, set off at what would a fast gallop on level ground.

Mario and Alma turned around, but Regina was already at some distance. She speedily disappeared, leaving the two young people disquieted and surprised.

As she went on, the amazon—her head bent down towards her horse's mane, her lips closed, and her eyes fixed—repeated, in a low tone:

"They love each other! They love each other! And I, who have loved him always, never suspected anything! Oh! Alma! Alma!"

In the glitter of her eyes, in the tones of her voice, there were furious menaces.

She soon arrived at the summit of the mountain; but instead of traversing the camp, she circled the plateau, and reentered the fort by a back entrance. As soon she had set foot on the ground, and thrown the bridle of her horse to a groom, she entered the buildings, and went into a fencing saloon at the back of them. Andrea Vitelli was at that moment meeting his principal subalterns, who came to him several times a day to receive his orders, or to inform him of the result of the expeditions which had been made in the mountains.

Andrea was seated in a large carved oaken chair, beside a map, in relief, of the configuration of the Apennines and the neighboring country. His eyes were fixed on a point in the neighborhood of the environs of Spoleto, on which he had stuck a pin.

When Regina entered, Andrea Vitelli raised his care laden brow.

He was no longer the sarcastic, careless-looking young man, whose acquaintance we made at the commencement of this narrative. Fifteen years had changed him much, and brought him close to his fortieth year. His black locks were somewhat grey over his forehead. He still possessed, however, a nervous, athletic form, and that bronzed tint, which, at an early age, he had acquired by an active life in the mountains. But numerous wrinkles now lined his forehead; and his eyebrows, which had become much thicker, gave a peculiar severity to his expression, which was naturally bold, and which the habit of command had rendered fixed and haughty.

Andrea Vitelli raised his head with a distraught air, and, having made to the young girl an affectionate sign, resumed his original attitude.

Regina approached, in the first place, five or six great dogs, which slept here and there upon a mat in the sun, and caressed them. Then she went to the table and gazed at the map, gradually drawing nearer to Andrea, and, at last, placing one hand upon his shoulder, asked:

"What you doing, my dear Signor?"

"You can see," replied Andrea, "I am studying."

"But what is that place then, upon which you have placed the pin?"

"It is a castle near Spoleto," he replied, knitting his great brows.

"A castle belonging to Count Ercole?"

"Yes."

"I thought that, thanks to your exertions, my dear Signor, Count Ercole no longer had any castle left."

"It is the last," said Andrea, in a deep voice "But why are you here? Why are you not with Alma?"

"Oh!" replied Regina. "I did not wish to disturb them."

"Disturb whom?"

"Alma and my noble cousin, Mario."

"What are they about?"

"They are walking together, side by side, arm in arm, and speaking so low that I could not hear them."

"Ah!" said Andrea, listening attentively.

"And then," continued Regina, "they are looking at each other so lovingly, oh, so very lovingly! But adieu, my dear uncle!"

Having said this, she lightly ran away. She was not ignorant that Alma could never become the wife of Mario without her uncle's consent, In fact, although Regina did not know the secret of her birth, she knew vaguely that the name of "niece," bestowed by Andrea Vitelli upon Alma, was only given in fun, or as a token of affection. She alone, Regina Vitelli, was the chief's only real niece, the daughter of that dear and unhappy sister, who had died in the flower of her age fifteen years since.

She was ignorant of the name of her father.

But she knew that Alma Vitelli, although she was loved for her angelic beauty, and although she herself, Regina, called her sister, was in reality the daughter of Count Ercole Vitelli, Andrea's mortal enemy.

Regina did not trouble herself about the manner in which she had come to the mountain. She knew that Alma had been carried off from her father at the most tender age, for the purpose, doubtless, of cruel vengeance; but that she had been so gentle, good, and affectionate, that the mountain chief had insensibly become attached to her, and had brought her up with the same care as Regina.

Andrea had frequently entertained the idea of sending the poor child back to her father; but so great was the charm which she exercised throughout the household, that he would have feared lest, in sending her away, he should be sending away his good angel.

Nevertheless, between his feelings of affection for her and the idea of allowing her to become the wife of Mario, there was a great gulf. Andrea could never consent to the marriage of his own son with the daughter of the man whom he hated more than anyone else in the world, and whom he had such good reasons to hate.

Regina, as will have been perceived, was not only a bold horsewoman, but had also some talent for the diplomatic arts. It was a clever maneuver to make Andrea share the suspicion which had entered her own breast.

She had succeeded to the utmost of her hopes. Andrea had already, possibly, some suspicion of this nascent love, and was so much the more disposed to receive fresh information on the subject.

When Regina had left her uncle's room, be began to walk about with impatient step, driving away with his foot the dogs that came across his path.

"She must go!" he said. "She exercises such an influence over everyone, that I believe I am no longer master of myself. I am weaker in her presence than any of them. I love her."

He stamped his foot on the ground impatiently. Then, as his face became clouded with a sad expression, he continued:

"My sister! My sister! Your death has no longer left me the right to pardon. I have promised to avenge you, and we keep the promises we make to people whom we have loved, and who are dead; but so long as this child is here, I feel as if some strange power has withheld my arm, and softened my resolution. She must go!"

At the moment when Andrea had formed this resolution, a subaltern, in charge of the advanced posts, entered, still covered with the dust of the road.

"What is it, Cosimo?" asked Andrea.

"Signor," replied the officer, "we have stopped, at two leagues from here, an old woman, who desires to speak with you."

"To speak with me?"

"Yes. She says that her name is Mercedes."

"Mercedes!" exclaimed Andrea. "Does this wretched creature come a second time to defy my justice?"

"What shall we do?" asked Cosimo.

"Bring her here," replied Andrea.

And then he crossed his arms upon his breast and awaited her.

II. The Guide

The duenna Mercedes had not come from Spoleto, but had that morning set out from a magnificent castle, situated not far from Narcia, a village near the mountains. This castle, to which we shall have again to refer, was the last of the domains of the old Prince of Monteleone inherited by Ercole Vitelli. It on the part of the map on which this castle figured that Andrea Vitelli had fixed the pin.

Mercedes had set out from this castle in the morning, mounted upon a mule, and with no other baggage than a large dark-colored parasol, to keep off the rays of the sun.

A peasant, whom she had induced with the offer of a large sum to serve as a guide, accompanied her, mounted on a small donkey. But instead of proceeding ahead of her, as is usual with guides, he had prudently trotted some fifty paces in the rear, and contented himself with pointing out the road, shouting out with all his might:

"Go to the right. Take the left."

This brave man was named Cocomero, and was a person held in much esteem in the village of Narcia, where his wife had bestowed on him almost innumerable progeny.

After a time, the beaten road dwindled into a mere path, which was soon, in its turn, lost in weeds, thickets, and rocks. The mountains were at hand, and the route of the travelers was soon constantly interrupted by rocks, torrents, and gorges of frightful depth.

The prudent Cocomero could no longer advance without the greatest difficulty; and although the heat was intense, his teeth chattered as if it had been far below freezing.

Each time that there appeared any uncertainty as to which direction she should proceed, Mercedes had to stop her mule and ask for information. Then she heard the feeble voice of Cocomero, murmuring through his chattering teeth:

"Go to the right," or "Turn to the left."

The fright of the poor fellow at last became so great, that he declared he no longer knew the road, and would not go a step further. It occurred to Mercedes that by promising him a good thrashing when he returned home, if he did not continue to act as her guide, she could persuade him to keep to his work; but this threat utterly failed to produce the desired effect, and Mercedes was obliged to promise him ten piasters in additional pay, if he would guide her to the nearest advance post of the people of the mountain.

Cocomero loved piasters. His avarice produced that which no amount of beating would; and the guide at last resolved to conduct Mercedes to a spot where she would be able to reach the advance post.

They proceeded on their road; Mercedes was far from sharing the fears of her companion, although she was by no means sure that her expedition would have the results which she hoped.

It was not the first time that she had penetrated the recesses of these terrible mountains. She had done so fourteen years earlier to ask Andrea for the return of Count Ercole's daughter. She had offered immense sums to the chief of the mountain bands in return for her, but had failed to induce him to consent. Then Mercedes, in the manner of the Parthians, who used to slay as they fled, had filled Andrea's heart with a lie which was very well calculated to become sooner or later the source of many tears. Leaning over the two cradles of the children, she had been prodigal with caresses to the daughter of Lucrezia Mammone, with the intention of thus making Andrea believe that it was the infant who was named Alma who was the legitimate daughter of Count Ercole.

It had been agreed between herself and the Count, who was passionately attached to his daughter, that she should act thus. Ercole had said:

"If he will not return my daughter to me, let her at least be happy, and have the foremost place in the house of my enemy."

The plot had perfectly succeeded; the lie had been completely established.

As the years had passed without anything occurring to explain the mistake, Regina had been brought up as the niece of Andrea, while Alma, whose place she possessed, passed as the daughter of the enemy, and only owed the kindness which Andrea displayed in respect to her to her angelic disposition.

In the course of time, the charm of Alma's goodness and beauty had made a wonderful impression upon the heart of the mountain chief; and it at length came to pass that he loved her almost as much as the brilliant Regina, whom he believed to be the daughter of his sister.

The duenna, as we have said, was already acquainted with the mountains, but Cocomero knew them also, and knew that they were full of danger for peasants. Many men from his village, who had ventured amongst the the Apennines, had disappeared so completely that their wives had never of them again. As they had not returned, they had been looked upon as dead, without anyone being able to say whether they had been murdered, or had fallen prey to the wolves. Now Cocomero felt no desire for such a melancholy a fate as this.

He kept as far behind his client as possible, and from time to time, looked back upon the soft landscape of the plain, filled with cattle and laborers, with regret. But at length the plain disappeared from view; and the travelers were hidden in a maze of tortuous gorges, whose savage magnificence was wrapped in gloomy solitude. The only things to be seen were huge masses of rock, deep and black abysses, immense fir trees, brambles, heath, and torrents. Now and then birds of prey flew from one rock to another, making hoarse cries like the yelping of foxes and the mewing of wild cats.

The mule and the donkey also seemed to advance with the utmost reluctance; the latter, especially, making melancholy brays, which the echo of the rocks repeated with mocking intonation, and which were particularly well calculated to make the wolves prick up their ears in the depths of the black forest of fir trees.

At length the travelers reached the summit of a small eminence, on which Cocomero came to determined halt, declaring that he would not move a step further, even if Mercedes should offer him sufficient money to buy the whole province. He then begged the duenna to recommend her soul to God, told her to keep always to the right, wished her a fortunate journey, and turned homewards, urging the donkey to the top of its speed.

The animal proceeded as its best pace, but had not advanced ten steps in its new direction, when the barrels of six muskets, which shone like silver in the sun, projected from above a rock which lay across the path and were directed with perfect unanimity towards the breast of the peasant.

The donkey came to a dead stop, and the unlucky Cocomero, opening his mouth and stretching out his arms, remained as motionless upon his donkey as Lot's wife when she turned into a pillar of salt.

He mutely implored the aid of his patron, Saint Francisco; but the saints of the plains were of no avail in the mountains.

At length, recovering the use of his tongue, he exclaimed:

"Mercy noble bandits! Mercy!" at the same time clasping his hands together, and even attempting to fall upon his knees on the donkey.

The men came forward. There were six of them, besides a leader, who was named Cosimo, and had in his hat an extraordinary long plume. He sported a great nose, and held a rapier of still greater comparative length.

"What do you do here, spy?" he said.

"I, a spy?" cried Cocomero, who already felt as if the cord were around his neck. "Holy Virgin! What a mistake! Ask that venerable lady there, and you will see!"

Mercedes, instead of taking flight, had drawn near; and the bandits could perceive, from the calmness of her expression that she had not come to the mountains without some distinct purpose.

"Woman," asked Cosimo, "for what reason have you come hither?"

"I have come to see your chief, Andrea Vitelli," she replied, in a calm voice.

"Very well," grumbled Cosimo, "but if this be a trick, my good woman, you will not escape by it; for we will conduct you to him ourselves."

"Proceed!" she said. "I am ready."

"And I, Signor bandit?" asked Cocomero. "Will you not let me go? I have nothing more to do here, I assure you; I have performed my task, and I should be glad to wish you a pleasant journey, and to descend to pray to the Madonna on your worship's behalf."

"Yes, descend!" roughly exclaimed Cosimo, at the same time pushing the peasant from off his donkey.

"What! You are going to deprive me of my donkey?" cried Cocomero, in despair. "My poor donkey! If you only knew, Signor bandit, how much I love my donkey! Oh! My donkey! My dear donkey! How can I return to the village without you?"

As he uttered these words Cocomero tore at his hair. One of the bandits approached him, quietly bound his wrists together, and then, wicked joker that he was, tied one end of the cord to the donkey's tail.

"Oh, great God!" cried the unfortunate Cocomero, "I see now that I am lost! Oh, let me go. noble bandits! Pray, let me go. Oh, think of my wife and children! What will Giovane, my dear wife, say?"

"Don't make so much noise," replied one of the brigands, named Torvocchiale. "Is your wife good-looking?"

"Ah, yes, Signor! As beautiful as the Madonna of Our Lady of Narcia."

"Well, then, you need not be anxious about her; she will find plenty willing to console her!"

Cocomero thought this a miserable pleasantry; but he did not care to say so to the fierce-looking Torvocchiale.

In the meantime Cosimo quietly mounted the donkey without allowing himself to be disquieted about the curious effect produced by his long legs, which almost touched the earth; then, spurring his steed, he said:

"donkey!"

The donkey set forth at a trot, forcing Cocomero, who was much less well provided with legs than Cosimo, to trot also. The unhappy wretch asked himself as he went along, whether it was possible that his dear wife, Giovane, would ever allow herself to be consoled by one of the neighbors. He mentally passed in review all the good-looking men of the village, and came to the conclusion that there was not one of them who was equal to him, Cocomero, either in body or mind.

The party proceeded at a good pace, and in less than two hours, arrived at the fort.

There Cocomero was detached from the donkey, and pushed into the stable, where he was to increase the number of the servants who performed the rough work of the fort, having first received a score or two of kicks from the bandits who were lounging about the yard.

In the meantime, Cosimo had informed Andrea of Mercedes' arrival.

IV. The Departure

Mercedes was introduced into Andrea's armory. A ray of sunlight traversed the vast hall, and fell upon the trophies of hunts and of war with which it was surrounded. The copper and the steel glittered in the shade with a stern, cold brilliance.

The duenna trembled as she entered.

Andrea gazed at her fixedly and, as he looked at this woman, after an interval of fourteen years, whom he had such good reasons to hate from his childhood, his blood boiled within him, and turned his forehead crimson.

"Why have you come here?" he asked, in a voice which made the duenna tremble.

At length she raised her eyes and looked at Andrea, which she had not ventured to do before. She was astonished to see how little change time had caused. He appeared to still be as lithe and vigorous as a young man. The only apparent changes were that his locks were grey on the temples, and the bronze of his complexion had acquired a deeper tint.

"I am the master here," continued Andrea.

"I know," replied Mercedes, in a quiet voice.

"This is the second time that you have come to the mountains to defy me."

"That is true," replied the duenna; then she added, whilst she trembled: "Alas! Signor, pardon me; I come not hither of my own will. I obey…"

"Well, what brings you here?"

"I come on behalf of Prince Ercole of Monteleone."

At the sound of this name the face of Andrea Vitelli took on so menacing an expression that Mercedes dared not continue.

Andrea passed his hand across his forehead.

"Continue," he said.

"The Prince is old," said Mercedes. "He is feeble and exhausted! He is no longer able to bear the weight of his misfortunes. He begs for your pity, Andrea. Ah! if you saw him now! He is such a miserable wretch, in spite of his titles and his fortune—his wife is dead! His poor wife, who died of grief after the loss of the daughter you carried off."

"Lucrezia Mammone is also dead!" said Andrea, in a deep voice.

The duenna remained silent.

"Continue," said Andrea. "I wish to hear all that you have to say."

"The Prince has lost everything because of you—ever thing—even his courage! He knows well that you possess a power beyond the power of men. He knows that gates of iron and walls of granite do nothing to check your steps; and he has seen you or your phantom, mute and mocking, resting upon your unsheathed sword behind the very curtains of his alcove…"

Andrea smiled.

"The Prince asks for mercy," continued the duenna, "and, oh, if you knew how he suffers—with sufferings beyond the power of human strength to bear! His castles have been burned down, his fields ravaged, and even the very grass under the windows of his palace destroyed. Insults attend him in public. All his friends have deserted him. Is it not much, Signor?"

"It is not enough," replied Andrea coldly.

The duenna covered her face with her hands, while Andrea said:

"You have not yet told me the real object of your visit."

"Ah, Signor, Signor!" cried Mercedes, clasping her hands together, "do not refuse me. It is the last hope of an old man. He entreats you to restore his daughter to him."

"His daughter!" interrupted Andrea, who seemed to reflect.

The duenna believed that the cause she pleaded was lost, and, as a final effort, said:

"In return for this favor, he will surrender to you half of what is still left to him."

Andrea drew himself up sternly, and shook his head with disdain.

"I want nothing of that man," he said.

"Alas!" murmured the duenna, anticipating a refusal.

Andrea interrupted her, saying, in a cold, severe voice:

"I consent, however, to restore his daughter to him."

Mercedes was almost on the point of collapsing, so great was her astonishment and joy.

"You shall take him back his child," continued Andrea, "but, at the same time, tell him that the account is not yet settled between us."

The smile faded from the duenna's face.

"The war between us is to the death."

The pale countenance of Mercedes bent beneath this menace. She was unable to make any reply. Her lips moved, but uttered no sound.

Andrea arose, and ordered a servant to send Alma to him.

The young girl entered the room with a smile upon her face, but when she saw Mercedes, her heart was filled with a secret terror.

Andrea played nervously with the handle of his dagger. It was painful to him to have to tell poor Alma that she was to be sent away from the mountain.

Alma was the joy and grace of his rude home; his cherished child, his tender consolation. Up to this hour, the great Demonio had never known how much he loved her. But now he suddenly perceived, in the depths of his being, that he loved her with all his heart.

But Regina—his pride—his real child. Was it not necessary that she should be happy? And was it not possible that the presence of Alma might convert this happiness into despair? For Regina loved Mario, and Mario had eyes only for Alma.

Andrea made an effort to speak.

"My child," he said, with a changed voice, "you are about to leave us."

"To leave you!" exclaimed the young girl, turning pale.

Andrea buried his face in his hands. He knew not what to say.

Alma awaited an explanation.

In the meantime, Mercedes, after having gazed attentively at the young girl, murmured:

"It is not she! It is not she! It is the daughter of Lucrezia. What must I do?"

Andrea's somber humor was not calculated to reassure her; but the dread of taking to the Prince any girl who was not his own daughter, inspired her with the courage of necessity.

While Andrea was shrinking from the interrogative glances of Alma, Mercedes approached him and murmured:

"Signor Andrea, Signor Andrea, are you sure that this young girl... Er... Are you sure that she is Count Ercole's daughter?"

Andrea gazed upon her coldly and sternly, as he replied:

"It was you yourself who told me so fourteen years ago."

The lie was, in fact, fourteen years-old, and was now bearing its fruits.

Mercedes, taken in her own snare, was filled with dismay. She saw that it impossible now to undeceive Andrea, and to explain to him the fraud which she had too successfully practiced upon him. She felt that it would be perfectly useless to make amends for her former treachery by an avowal of the truth, since Andrea would not fail to regard the avowal itself as a falsehood. But the dread which she entertained of Andrea was the chief cause of her remaining silent. It only remained for her to act as well as she could under the circumstances, and to take Alma, as she could not have the Prince of Monteleone's true daughter, Regina. She reflected, also, that Alma would at least be a hostage.

Andrea had resumed his sad and meditative attitude.

In the meantime, poor Alma, pale and tearful, waited for Andrea to explain the resolution which was about to so suddenly change the whole course of her existence, and separate her from all she loved in the world.

The leader of the bandits at length raised his head.

"My child," he repeated, "you are about to leave us. It must be so. You are not ignorant of the fact that you are the daughter of the Prince—of the Prince of Monteleone?"

"I have been told so," murmured the young girl.

"It is the truth, my poor child!"

"Ah, no!" exclaimed Alma, bursting into sobs. "I have no other father but you!"

Andrea was deeply moved as he murmured in reply:

"My child! You are in reality my daughter, and with all my heart I feel for you as a father; but I have no right to refuse to restore you to your family, which asks for you."

Alma looked at him fixedly, as if she understood that in speaking thus, he was not giving his real reasons.

"You should have restored me, then, fourteen years ago," she said, as her tears fell fast. "I should not then have been accustomed to live here—to see you constantly—to love you!"

And she paused, rendered speechless by her tears.

Andrea was painfully aware of the justice of this reproach; and although he was a man who had long been hardened against weaknesses of all sorts, he could not resist the anguish which now oppressed him.

He threw his arms round Alma's waist, and kissed her forehead with passion.

"My child," he said, repressing his emotion as well as he could, "in acting thus, I am but performing an act of duty. I shall ever remember you, and we may love each other although apart, but we *must* part."

He interrupted himself.

The years of Alma's infancy passed before his eyes, which were no longer susceptible to tears. It seemed to him as if he were about to dismiss from his roof the beneficent genius of domestic happiness.

He knew that it would be so, but, controlling his voice as well as he could, he continued:

"Alma, even before the arrival of this woman, your departure had been decided."

Mercedes listened with the utmost attention; for she perceived that there was some mystery concealed beneath Andrea's words; but what it was, she could not divine.

Alma, utterly overcome, could only weep helplessly.

"At least," she murmured, "send for my sister, that I may take leave of her!"

Andrea sent for Regina, but it was impossible to find her. In order to leave Andrea to ponder upon her words as deeply as possible, she had, immediately after her return, taken Mario for a walk in the environs of the fort.

This was an additional affliction for Alma, who loved Regina as a sister.

In spite of what had passed during the morning, her heart, which was incapable of entertaining any feeling of rancor, was deeply afflicted at the idea of departing without giving a farewell kiss to the companion of her youth.

"Every misfortune comes upon me at once," she murmured.

Andrea, anxious to shorten this painful scene, summoned Cosimo, and said to him:

"You will conduct these two ladies, with good escort, to the plain."

"I am ready," said Cosimo.

"Now, my child," said the leader of the bandits, "adieu!"

Alma took Andrea's hand and kissed it, watering it with her tears. Then, blushing and confused, she said, in a voice stifled with sobs:

"You will say farewell to Regina for me?"

"I will," replied Andrea.

"And to Mario?"

Andrea made no reply to this request but, turning to Mercedes, he said:

"Now!" and he spoke in a voice which made her tremble, "tell your master that he had best summon up all his courage; for this child, whom I love, has hitherto been his shield; but now, only now, my vengeance will commence."

Mercedes bowed her tall figure, and made no reply.

"Come, my child," she said, taking Alma by the hand.

The feet of the latter seemed unable to raise themselves from the ground.

Then Mercedes whispered gently in her ear:

"Your father awaits you, and he loves you."

Alma trembled. Some hidden part of her soul vibrated within her. She followed the duenna and they left the building, followed by Cosimo.

Andrea felt as if his heart would break as he watched Alma depart. It seemed to him as if a portion of himself was being torn away. He hastened to close the door so he could hide his grief.

The men making up the escort were ready in the courtyard.

A grotesque incident occurred in the midst of this melancholy scene.

Mercedes' guide, poor Cocomero, suddenly appeared, mounted on his donkey. Cosimo, thinking that his chief included him in those who were to be conducted back to the plain, had restored to him his donkey and his liberty.

Cocomero, intoxicated with joy, behaved on his donkey as if he were possessed, making the air resound with his joyous shouts.

"Hurrah for liberty!" he cried, "It shall not be said that I sold my donkey for drink money! Hurrah! Hurrah for liberty! I shall see my dear wife again, before any of the neighbors have had time to console her. Hurrah for liberty, Signor bandits!"

The donkey, partaking in its master's joy, at the same time made the air resound with formidable bray.

Mercedes mounted her mule, and took Alma on the crupper. The escort, consisting of six men and Cosimo, rested their muskets over their left shoulders, and set on their way.

They traversed the camp, Alma still weeping bitterly. As soon as it became generally known by the people of the mountain that Alma was about to leave them, there was nothing to be heard but a concert of complaints and lamentations. Women, old men, and children accompanied her to the edge of the plateau. Some kissed her hand, others the hem of her dress, and others even her charming little feet. Had it not been for the escort, they would have torn the duenna into pieces, and carried Alma back in triumph.

When the procession reached the edge of the plateau there was a long leave taking, mingled with many tears. For as far as it was possible the warm-hearted people followed Alma with their eyes, as she proceeded along the winding mountain path, waving their handkerchiefs, their hats, and their sticks until she was lost to view.

The affection displayed by these poor people was some consolation to Alma's grief. Her tears ceased to flow, and with eyes fixed, and open mouth, she swayed with the motions of the mule, scarcely conscious of where she was.

As she thus yielded herself up to that dreamy state of inertness so common with those who are worn out from suffering, her eyes were suddenly struck by a distant apparition—a sort of vision, a strange silhouette, which ran and leaped from one rocky peak to another, and stood out in a dark outline against the brilliant azure of the mountain sky.

On looking more attentively, she recognized the strange personage whom, in common with the people of the mountain, she had called the *Woman in grey*.

The Woman in grey seemed to follow attentively the progress of the escort. Her attitude was no longer that strange air of indecision which had characterized it on the morning when Alma had met her by the spring. She evidently took a deep interest in the proceedings of the escort, since she followed it always at the same distance, in spite of the difficulties of the ground, which was rough, and crisscrossed with torrents.

Several times, Alma, when she had descended for a time from the mule to ease her limbs, wearied by its fatiguing trot, fancied that she saw the Woman in grey leaning over the traces left by her feet in the sand.

This curious apparition not escaped the notice of the people of the mountain, who re-entered their tents, saying:

"What is that sorceress about? Alas! Alas! We shall no longer be able to protect our dear Alma against evil!"

Two hours after Alma's departure, Andrea was still in his armory, his elbows resting on the table, and his face buried in his hands.

He dreamed of the child who was no longer there, and his soul, traversing the long slope of memory, found in its course other griefs, older and more bitter.

"Poor Lucrezia!" he exclaimed, with bitterness. "Dead at twenty!"[13]

And he pressed his face with yet more painful force upon his two hands.

At that moment the door of chamber was noiselessly opened.

Regina, light as a bird, entered on the tips of her toes.

The leader of the bandits did not perceive her. She did not dare to disturb his reverie.

A second time the door opened; but this time it was thrown wide open violently.

Mario appeared on the threshold.

He was pale, and supported himself on the shining barrel of his fowling-piece; his clenched fingers seemed as if they would enter the very iron.

"Father!" he said, in a voice in which there was mingled anger and pain, "is it true that Alma will no longer live with us?"

"It is true!" replied Andrea.

Regina, who had glided behind a war trophy which concealed her, wore a strange smile on her face.

---

[13] Andrea's memory is somewhat faulty since she was "scarcely seventeen" in 1840 when she committed suicide to save the Vitellis's honor. But then Féval is often off by a year or two in the continuity of his narratives.

"She has quit the mountain," continued Mario, "and has done so by your order?"

"By my order!" replied Andrea, raising his haughty countenance.

The butt of Mario's gun struck heavily against the floor, and the trophies with which the walls were covered made a metallic clamor. The eyes of the young man were alight with flame.

"By Heavens, then! If you were not my father…"

"Well?" said Andrea.

Foam came to the mouth of Mario, who, in his blind rage, closed his fist with a menacing air.

Andrea Vitelli loaded one of the richly inlaid pistols, which always lay on his table.

Mario raised his carbine.

All this was likely enough to occur, in the wild state of manners which prevailed amongst the people of the mountain.

Regina looked on curiously. Her heart did not beat a pulse faster than usual.

"Go!" said Andrea, dashing his pistol against a marble slab.

Mario let fall his gun, and left the room with a gesture of menace.

Regina, crouching in her corner, hidden in the shade, knit her brows, and murmured:

"How he loved her!"

Then the smile returned to her lips, which had now become pale, as she thought: *I am beautiful; and now that she has gone, he will love me!*

V. False Joy

Two leagues from the Apennines, on the side of Narcia, was a large and beautiful valley. Some pools, the waters of which reposed in the midst of this vast hollow, lent transparency to the landscape. Especially when the setting sun threw its light upon them, these waters lent an indescribable air of splendor and mystery to the scene.

Anyone who has visited the basaltic rocks of the isles of the north, and traversed their infinite colonnades, through which dash the broken, furious waves; anyone who has visited the caverns, tapestried with stalactites, of Belgium or Germany, will be able to immediately comprehend the principle of the mythologies of Greece, Scandinavia, or Egypt.

And this principle will appear as a sudden revelation. Watch, on the other hand, the vast marsh pools which sleep at the bottom of a valley, at the hour when the setting illumines their dormant waters, which still burn brightly, while all around them sits in gloom and shade, and you will understand the mythology of those good people—the fairies of the villages.

The valley of Fonte-Righhi borrowed from the changing light of its waters that mysterious character of which we have just spoken.

An immense Gothic castle stood at one of the extremities of this valley, and added further to the somber and majestic of its aspect.

At the decline of day, when its black towers stood out boldly against the blood-red clouds of the horizon, the valley, heavy with shade, took on an appearance so strange and fantastic, that travelers could not traverse it without fear.

There was an inconceivable sadness about that monotonous mirage, on which was painted the colossal figure of the castle. The superstition of the people of the valley had placed crowds of phantoms behind the mournful looking walls, and along the desolate margins of the vast pools. It was scarcely possible to behold that scene without feeling as if the air was heavy with misfortune. This castle was Count Ercole's last possession —the only one that the vengeance of his enemies had left him.

It occupied an excellent position on the highest ground of the neighboring country. Its walls were proof against any assault, and in that age of mighty fortresses, the enormous depth of its moats was impressive.

It was thither that Ercole Vitelli, overwhelmed with ennui and chagrin, by fatigue and terrors which were incessantly renewed, driven from all his estates by his pitiless enemy, and disturbed even at Spoleto, in his own palace, had fled as if it was an asylum where he might be sheltered from any surprise. This castle bore the name of the neighboring village, Narcia, which had since then grown into a town.

Day night the drawbridge of the castle was raised; and no one was admitted into it unless his name, his place of abode, and the object of his visit were well known. In spite of all these precautions, however, Prince Ercole scarcely dared to close his eyes. He passed the nights without sleep, and never took a morsel of food till his taster had swallowed two mouthfuls in his presence.

Life at the castle of Narcia was very, very dreary. No one was to be seen there but soldiers and servants. The Count's courtiers had all fled.

Anyone who possessed a fortune preferred his liberty to a weary existence in the company of a Prince prematurely aged by misfortune, and continually overwhelmed by terror.

The number of gentlemen who remained faithful to the old Count of Spoleto was not considerable. There were three of them, and all three were so necessitous that it was not difficult to guess the reason of their devotion. One of them was named Capitan, another Tiberio Fanferluizzi, and the third Pasquale Contarini.

We made their acquaintance at the commencement of this narrative, on the Piazza of Spoleto. Capitan was then the leader of Count Ercole's assassins; and Tiberio Fanferluizzi and Pasquale Contarini wore chains of gold on their velvet doublets, which had long since found their way into the hands of the usurers of the domain of Saint Peter.

Besides these gentlemen, the Count of Spoleto had no other companion but Mercedes. The duenna seemed bound to the existence of Ercole by some mysterious tie, which had long been a topic of conversation in the surrounding country. Many years before, some unknown hand had raised a corner of the veil concealing this mystery. Dark rumors had the taken the place of the malicious insinuations to which this connection between the Count and the duenna had formerly given rise.

Whispers were uttered about some crime—a horrible, cowardly crime. Public infamy fastened upon the name of Ercole Vitelli. This rendered his life still more desolate and sad.

For a long time he had with him his wife, Bianca Orsini, an amiable and worthy woman, whose devotion had been his solace. But Bianca had died of fear.

On a gloomy winter evening, the eve of some saint's day, she had been alone in the chapel of the castle, when a stone had been raised at the bottom of the choir where there was no light. A specter had arisen, in the form of the Prince of Monteleone, according to some; in that of Lucrezia Mammone, according to others; for both had been victims of the Countess's husband. Bianca fell prostrate, never to rise again. The story of the specter was, perhaps, an invention; but it was certainly true that she had been found dead on the cold flagstones of the chapel.

The secret griefs by which he had been overwhelmed, had seriously affected Ercole Vitelli's health.

His daughter torn from him;[14] his wife dead of fright; his domains laid waste—all these things had shattered his constitution. Although he had not yet attained his sixtieth year, he could easily have been taken for four-score. His head bowed down upon his breast, and its naked crown, around which still hung a few tufts of white hair, but nothing about him inspired the reverence due the elderly.

His face was wrinkled; he walked supported by a stick and almost bent double. A characteristic trait of his premature old age was visible in the shrugging up of his shoulders, which gave Count Ercole the appearance of a man who feared every moment to see the roof of his house come tumbling upon his head.

It will readily be allowed that, in such a state things as this, the result of Mercedes' expedition was a matter of much importance to the Count of Spoleto. In fact, the

---

[14] Féval appears to have forgotten the existence of Fiamma, Ercole's elder daughter, mentioned in the Prologue, Chapter II.

answer of Andrea Vitelli would determine whether he should have solace in the last years of his life, or be the victim of unmitigated misery.

He passed the greater part of the day in a lofty chamber in one of the castle's turrets; and from there sweeping the surrounding country with his glance, he awaited the return of Mercedes with the anxiety of a condemned criminal.

The hours of the day had passed one by one, and Count Ercole's forehead had begun to cloud with despair, when he perceived, not far from the castle, a woman mounted upon a mule, advancing toward the drawbridge. It was Mercedes. A young girl clothed white sat upon the crupper behind the duenna.

The Count uttered a cry of joy. Andrea had returned his child to him! Andrea had accepted the proposal which he had sent Mercedes to make to him. He descended as quickly as his age and weakness permitted him.

Mercedes and Alma entered.

"My daughter!" cried the old man, pressing Alma to heart. "My child, for whom I have so long wept!"

Alma allowed herself to be embraced by the old man; but, although she was convinced that she was in the presence of her real father, she did not experience any of that emotion of tenderness which she would have wished to feel.

After having yielded to the first impulse of his joy, the Count fell back a step and gazed upon the young girl with the utmost earnestness.

Gradually an expression of doubt and anxiety stole over his countenance, and replaced the gleam of pleasure which had made him suddenly appear twenty years younger.

"She does not resemble her mother at all," he first murmured.

Then he added, casting a terrified look upon the duenna:

"She looks like... Oh! She looks like..."

"...Lucrezia Mammone," said Mercedes slowly.

As she uttered these words, she retired to the other end of the hall, leaving poor Alma by herself, astonished at this reception.

Ercole followed the duenna with trembling steps.

"She is not the right daughter," he exclaimed, in broken tones.

"It is Lucrezia's daughter," replied the duenna.

"Ah!" burst forth the Count. "Why? Why?"

His eyes gleamed with angry fire.

"My lord," replied the duenna, who trembled, "I have tried my utmost to obey you, but we are the victims of our own deceits. Andrea believed that your Regina was his niece, and that Alma was your daughter. God's vengeance pursues us."

"God? God?" growled the old man. "It is you who has blundered."

"When I formerly deceived Andrea on the subject, it was on your orders."

"You should have undeceived him."

"He would not have believed me. When we sow falsehoods, we must expect to reap errors."

"Calamity! Calamity!" murmured the old man, whose head bent wearily towards the ground.

"Ought I not to have brought this young girl?" asked Mercedes, timidly.

"Yes, you were right in doing so," replied the old man at the same time fixing his gaze upon Alma, who stood where the duenna had left her, with eyes cast down upon the ground, and unable to hear a word of the conversation, which had been carried on in a low tone.

An expression or cunning came to the lips of the Count, as he continued:

"Yes, you have done right in bringing this young girl to me. If Andrea will not restore my legitimate daughter to me, I at least have his sister's child in my hands. She is a hostage; and if he does not abandon his attacks on me, I shall know how to avenge myself."

He then resumed his natural tone, and, forcing a smile to his face, said:

"Welcome! Welcome, my daughter; and bless providence, which has at last restored you to the bosom of your family. Your presence here will bring happiness to this desolate house. In the hope of your arrival we have given orders for a *fête* in honor of your return. Come!"

He thereupon took her by the hand and led her into a vast salon where some gentlemen and officers of the fort were walking and conversing. Among them the reader will recognize three old friends, Tiberio Fanferluizzi, Capitan, and Pasquale Contarini.

The passage of years had changed them but little. Tiberio had retained all his grace of person. His locks, as red as ever, were curled as of yore; the perfumes which exhaled from his person were as rich as formerly; and he had not a bow or a knot less, from his shoes to his frill.

It must be admitted, however, that this flamboyance was much faded, due to the emptiness of his purse and the hardness of the times.

Capitan, for his part, was still more formidable looking than when he been present at the duel between Andrea and his two comrades.

As for Pasquale Contarini, with the exception that his nose had changed from red to violet, he was still the same; and the change of color in that member was so far from injuring his appearance, that it might fairly be said to have enhanced it, since it lent a new and joyous brilliance to his appearance.

At the entrance of Alma a murmur of admiration ran throughout the salon. The Count presented her as his daughter, and received the congratulations of the whole company. The brave Capitan himself, who in general paid but little attention to the fair sex, swore, by half-a-dozen devils and saints, that the Prince's daughter was as bright and brilliant as a newly scoured cuirass.

Pasquale Contarini declared that was as graceful as a flask of Saint Geneze, the neck of which is as graceful as the pistil of a flower, and pours forth floods of rubies.

Tiberio Fanferluizzi almost fell into a fainting fit at the sight of her, and endeavored to recall to mind some of his best sonnets to the moon. He scratched his red locks, devoted his memory to Satan, and swore that he would compose that very evening a new sonnet, such as Petrarch [15] himself had never equaled.

After having undergone a flood of compliments framed according to the fashion of the age, which demanded that they should be full of emphasis and allusions to heathen gods and goddesses, and after having been compared to Venus rising from the sea, to Diana, to the moon, to the stars, to the sun, Alma was conducted to the supper room, where smoked a repast of the most splendid description, lit by a hundred silver candelabra.

---

[15] Francesco Petrarca (1304-1374), Italian scholar and poet who was one of the earliest humanists. His rediscovery of Cicero's letters is often credited with initiating the 14th-century Renaissance.

The Count had stored in his castle at Narcia all that remained to him of his ancient wealth.

But all this magnificence, far from being the source of any pleasure to the young girl, only caused her to make sad comparisons between her present and past life. It reminded her bitterly of the simple mountain repasts which she had shared Mario, Regina, and Andrea Vitelli—Mario, whom she loved, without confessing it even to herself, Regina, her dearly cherished sister, and Andrea, that noble chieftain, who so good even in his pride, and whom she had so long respected as her father!

She longed for the moment when she should be allowed to leave the table; to retire to the chamber allotted to her; and to give herself up to her thoughts. But it was the habit to drink deeply at Ercole's castle, where, indeed, there was little other amusement to be found but what might consist in the pleasures of the table. The repast was therefore a prolonged one, and the conversation after a time became animated. It turned upon the events which had recently occurred in the neighborhood.

"Gentlemen," said an officer of the fort, "I can myself give you some news. Last week, on returning from Spoleto, I encountered, or rather, I perceived at a distance, on the plain, Bel Demonio, with his twelve Africans."

"Bel Demonio!" exclaimed several. "What nonsense!"

The officer twirled his moustache, as he cried:

"By Heavens! I only tell you what I saw."

"Well, well, Signor officer," said the most curious, "we believe you; but tell us more about it."

Alma opened her eyes; for she was as astonished to hear Bel Demonio spoken of in the castle as she had been to hear him spoken of in the mountain. The forehead of the Prince had, in the meantime, contracted. A vague expression of terror pervaded his countenance.

"By the holy rood!" cried Capitan, whose utterances were becoming thick, "I should be glad to meet him some night by the light of the moon, and measure with him the length of our swords!"

The conversation having taken a valorous turn, could not—among such soldiers as those present—be easily allowed to drop. Oaths and boastful expressions flew about from one end of the table to the other. At the same time, the name of Bel Demonio was constantly mentioned in the course of the conversation; and it seemed that no one could give an accurate account of this fantastic personage, who, according to one of the mountain ballads, was *as fair a girl, and as strong as a devil.*

No one could positively assert that he had seen him face to face; but each had his anecdote—of castles burned to the ground, of iron gates broken, as if by enchantment, and of strange apparitions, which gave to this wonderful being an extraordinary, supernatural aspect.

The officers and gentlemen continued to drink. Only the Count had, for some time, left his glass empty, and seemed to have fallen into one of his somber reveries.

In the meantime Mercedes, who understood that it impossible Alma to remain any longer amidst a crowd of men who were accustomed to prolonging their libations far into the night, took her by the hand, and conducted her into the chamber which had been prepared for her; and having offered her any assistance she might require, which Alma had declined, she wished her good night, and retired.

Alma's chamber was situated on the first story in the turret on the west side of the castle. It was richly furnished, but in a somewhat antique style, which was not calculated to give the mind of a young girl agreeable impressions. A deeply recessed window lit the chamber, which was ornamented with ancient draperies, the finest production of the looms of Flanders.

Alma did not feel at ease. She looked at the fastening of the door, and pushed two enormous bolts into their sockets. Then, somewhat reassured, she drew aside the curtains and opened the window. It was a magnificent moonlit night, and the valley, bathed in the moon's melancholy splendor, was visible throughout its whole extent. Outside, all was still and calm; whilst within, the hoarse echoes of the orgy sometimes penetrated even to the ears of the young girl.

Alma leaned upon the balcony. She gazed upon the magnificent scene spread out before her. Sometimes her eyes rested upon the crests of the Apennines, where she had left all that was dear to her; sometimes they wandered over the neighboring countryside, sadly comparing these unknown scenes with those which her memory brought back to her so vividly. At the foot of the turret extended a moat tapestried with herbs and shrubs.

The rays of the moon plunged into the midst of this foliage and water, where, from time to time, some bird of prey darted forth to secure its victim, breaking the calm mirror of the water, and for a minute, making the pale rays of the moon dance upon its surface.

Farther on was a rampart covered with short herbage, on which a sentinel slumbered, resting on his musket. Farther on still were the fields, the valleys, and the great marshland, mute and mystical. The whole scene, at first glance, seemed as lonely as it was silent; but, as she gazed around her, Alma was witness to a spectacle which should not have escaped the eyes of the sentinel.

A shadowy form had climbed the exterior rampart, and was gazing attentively at the castle, as if it wished to study its configuration and its outworks. This motionless and vague form seemed to be covered with dark-colored garments, and to be posed in an attitude full of melancholy.

Alma gazed and gazed; and the more she gazed, the more she became convinced, with inexpressible astonishment, that this strange figure was identical to the apparition had surprised her near the fountain, during her last conversation with Regina. She saw that it was the woman whom the country people called the Woman in grey!

Alma asked herself what strange reason caused this woman to follow her thus—what singular attraction drew her to follow her steps?

To this question she could give no reply.

But the presence of the poor woman, far from increasing her fears, somewhat reassured her. It was pleasant for her, desolate as she then felt, to find that someone was interested in her. She was no longer alone; some ne was watching over her. Someone very powerless, no doubt, but how weak is the tuft of grass which sometimes saves the unhappy wretch, carried away by the current.

Alma took her handkerchief and waved it. The poor woman immediately perceived it, and, stretching out her arm, sent toward Alma a thousand kisses.

The young girl replied to this by a gracious inclination of the head, and then, pointing towards the sentinel, signified that she thought it prudent for the Woman in grey to depart. The poor woman, however, still remained.

Being afraid for her, Alma closed her window. Only then did the Woman in grey, with regret, slowly depart.

With her face pressed closely to the window, Alma long followed the strange woman with her eyes. When she could no longer see her, she let the curtains fall back upon the casement, and went down upon her knees to pray, and then she retired to rest.

Who can explain the mysterious logic which controls thoughts of young girls? The presence of the strange woman was to Alma a message from the mountain.

When Alma fell asleep, she dreamed of the image of Mario Vitelli, gracious and smiling, sitting at her bedside.

VI. Marina

Despite the emotions that had shaken her all day, Alma slept profoundly.

When she awoke it was late morning and the rays of the sun slipping between the curtains, gilded the Flemish paintings covering the walls.

For a moment, she followed those fantastic hunting scenes, in which we so frequently see a stag bearing a cross between its horns, and Saint Hubert kneeling before it, and the famous doe, which has for so many ages been flying ahead of the eager dogs, which are never able to catch it.

Alma leaped from her bed and ran to the window, from whence she saw the valley, golden with the rays of the sun, and freed from the mists of the night, spread out before her like a painted panorama.

The blue crests of the Apennines appeared at the end of the valley, holding the eyes with calm satisfaction. Poor Alma sighed at the sight of the mountains.

The keen, sharp air of the Abruzzi pleased her more than the warm breath of the valleys.

And then, all those whom she loved were there—Mario, Andrea, and Regina.

She said her prayers, started to dress, and then rose and buried herself in her bed for a moment, to be the better able to collect her thought, and turn them towards the absent ones.

Some light taps at the door aroused her from her reverie.

"Who is it?" she asked.

"I, Mademoiselle."

"And who are you?"

"Marina."

The voice was soft and youthful, and Alma, reassured, arose and unbolted the door.

Although she did not know Marina, she allowed her to enter; and, in fact, it would have been difficult for anyone to have been frightened by Marina.

She was a young peasant girl of fifteen or sixteen years of age, as brown as a nut and as red as a cherry, and with the most charming eyes.

She had come to aid Alma in her toilet. She acquitted herself very well in her duties as lady's maid; this being a qualification common to the women of all Countries.

Alma, charmed with having so pretty a creature for an attendant, gave a cordial reception to Marina, whose tongue was easily unloosed, and who forthwith began to gossip without cease.

Far from checking her, Alma encouraged her to go on, by now and then asking questions; and she thus learned some of the details of the interior of the castle, and the mode of life its inhabitants.

It appeared that life in the castle was truly melancholy. The persons dwelling in it were, for the most part, soldiers, who spent the morning tending their horses and furbishing their arms, then spent the rest of the day drinking. Others were engaged in military exercises in the courtyard, practicing with the saber, the pike, or the musket.

And frequently these amicable contests—carried on as they were by persons naturally disposed to quarrel, and excited by wine—ended in serious combat.

As for Count Ercole, he was an old man of a very singular character. He passed almost the whole day shut up in his rooms, overwhelmed by bitter reflections, of which no one knew the cause.

Before dinner he was wont to walk the ramparts, examining the open country and the distant mountains with anxious eyes.

At dinner, he gathered around him his officers and a few gentlemen, who passed more than three-fourths of their lives at the castle, some from vanity, and others from necessity.

Signor Tiberio Fanferluizzi, for example, could never have consented to live in the intimacy of gentlemen of a lower class; and he therefore adhered very closely to the house of his good friend Ercole, the hereditary Prince of Monteleone.

As for Pasquale Contarini, the cellar and kitchen of the castle had incomparable merits in his eyes and, that he might be the better able to appreciate them, he had definitively taken up his abode in a comfortable chamber in the east turret.

Marina's tongue, as it rattled on, did not spare Capitan, who had also taken up his abode in the fort; and, indeed, he was a precious man to have in an isolated mansion, exposed to the attacks of mountain bandits.

Capitan understood military maneuvers better than anyone, and used them and abused them in such a manner, that, if not been for the protection afforded him by the Count, the soldiers under him would have turned him out of doors.

The clamor of his great rapier, which was continually heard banging against the walls on the stairs, was music to the Count, and a veritable solace to his heart.

He relied upon the vigilance of Capitan to protect his threatened life. After having drunk their morning cup, the three gentlemen of whom we speak would gaily mount their steeds, and proceed to entertain themselves in the cabarets of Spoleto or its environs. It was rarely, however, that the dinner-hour did not find them back at the castle.

The rest of the evening was spent in drinking, games of chance, or conversation.

It was then that Capitan, choosing a favorable moment, would recount feats of daring sufficient to make the hair of his auditors stand erect—feats of daring, however, which were somewhat problematical, and for the reality of which he alone could vouch.

"And is that the only way in which people pass their lives here?" asked Alma.

"Before," replied Marina, "they used to hunt; but since a strange encounter that happened to the Count as he was returning from the forest one evening, there is no more hunting. The dogs have not left their kennel for six months, and have become dull and fat. Even their keeper has grown a stomach as big as a Dutchman's."

"But what was this thing, then, that happened to the Count?"

"Oh, a very strange thing, of which people talked throughout the whole country. He encountered Bel Demonio, mounted on his African horse and accompanied by his twelve Moorish followers, clothed in white mantles."

"Always this Bel Demonio," murmured Alma to herself, who became thoughtful. "And what did he do to the Count?" she asked, aloud.

"No one knows for certain, Mademoiselle. Some say that he struck the Count with his scimitar; others, that he seized him by the hair and dragged him for a mile along the sward; and others, that he whispered in his ears three words, which left him as mute and pale as the marble statues in the palace of Spoleto."

Her toilet finished, Alma followed Marina to the refectory. The Count received her affectionately, and kissed her forehead. Alma thought that could perceive in the old man's eyes a more genuine tenderness than that which he had shown towards her on the previous evening.

The fact was that Alma diffused around her a charm so great and irresistible, that the old man involuntarily succumbed to its influence. When he saw her enter, fresh and radiant as a morning in spring, he forgot that he kept her as a hostage, and, if need be, as an instrument of vengeance.

The old fort, with its thick and gloomy walls, seemed to him less gloomy and melancholy since Alma had entered it. The presence of this child had the same effect upon his heart as a refreshing dew has upon arid ground.

As for the young girl, she felt no other sympathy for the Count than that which is naturally inspired by the sight of an old man bowed down by misfortune and melancholy, and she reproached her heart for its coldness towards he whom she believed to be her father.

At breakfast she exerted herself to appear affectionate towards the old man, and the naive graces which she displayed had the effect of completely gaining his heart.

After the repast, Ercole took Alma by the hand, and said:

"Come, my child, and I will show you around the castle; you will perceive, I hope, that you will pass a pleasanter life here than amidst the barren mountains, where a fatal misunderstanding so long detained you."

He led her along the ramparts, and conducted her to a narrow garden enclosed by the high walls of the barracks, the stables, and the dwellings. These walls were tapestried by ivy plants a hundred years-old, the somber verdure of which gave a tone of sadness to the spot. A few sickly trees grew here and there, pale and weak, like poor prisoners deprived of air and sunlight.

The grass grew discolored beneath the shadow of these melancholy trees; there was nothing in the whole garden, in fact, which was calculated to refresh either the heart or the eyes. Everything about it was dull and desolate, and resembled a cemetery more than a garden.

As Count Ercole wandered, his head bowed down and with trembling steps, amidst this melancholy scene, one might have supposed that he was a corpse, seeking his own tomb.

He bade Alma sit upon a rustic bench, and, gazing in silence on the countenance which reminded him of Lucrezia Mammone, he heaved a sigh.

Ercole Vitelli was not one of those old men who can look back upon the past and smile. Everything recalled to his mind some bitter or mournful thought, which he vainly attempted to drown. His memory was his most cruel enemy; and, unfortunately for him, one cannot murder memory.

"Ah!" he said to himself, "if at least I had beside me my daughter, my real daughter! And to think that only a few leagues separate me from her, in whose young and pure existence I should revive, and that I have not the power to go myself, sword in hand, to demand her of that Andrea, Oh! To know this is to suffer twenty deaths!"

And the unhappy old man grew pale with rage at the sense of his own weakness, and with the remorse which tore his heart at the remembrance of his past career.

"You suffer, my father?" said Alma, gently drawing closer to him.

"No! No!" replied Ercole. "I was thinking of you, my child, and my heart bled at the thought of the dreary life you must have led amongst those people of the mountain."

"I was not unhappy there," rejoined Alma, "for everyone was kind to me."

"But you were alone and had no young person of your own age as a companion."

"Pardon me, father, but I had a sister."

"A sister?"

"Yes. Regina, Andrea's niece. We called each other sister, and we loved each other. The time passed very, very pleasantly, and I can assure you that our days were never darkened by the least cloud of sorrow."

"Well, well, I can imagine that," replied the old man, dissimulating the pleasure he experienced in speaking of his daughter. "But your sister Regina, did they treat her as kindly as they treated you?"

"Oh!" exclaimed Alma with a celestial smile. "Regina as the spoiled child of the house; Signor Andrea loves her as much, and perhaps more, than his own son, Mario."

"He is a happy man," murmured the old man to himself; before adding aloud: "She must be very charming, then, if everyone loves her so?"

"Everyone obeys her," said Alma, "and, indeed, they must, for, charming as she is, she wears at her waist two little pistols, of she would make good use if anyone ill-treated her. Oh! She can be demon when she likes!"

"Indeed?"

"Yes! Everyone must obey her least gesture, her every word."

"How amusing," cried the old man, for the first time for twenty years bursting into a hearty laugh.

"If you were there with her," said Alma, "you would obey her as everybody else does."

"I can well believe it."

"Horses, dogs, and arms; those are the things she cares about."

"Horses, you say? Does she ride, then?"

"All day long and is daring as a man."

"But a girl might run into some danger... An accident easily occurs. She is watched, at least?"

"No! She always goes alone. She will not allow anyone to follow her. If they were to do that, she would think that they were attempting to interfere with her independence, of which she is very proud."

"Poor young girl" said the old man, with a sad smile. "I do not know why I am so interested in her. And you said she is named...?"

"Regina."

"And is she pretty?"

"With the beauty of an angel and a demon."

"You yourself are charming," said the old man, kissing her forehead.

"Only," said Alma, with a meaningful smile on her lips and a sarcastic glance, "there is something about Regina which frightens me."

"Frightens you?"

"Yes, indeed."

"What is it, then?"

"Her eyes."

"I do not understand you."

"Oh! When Regina, who is generally so good, becomes angry, her glance is so threatening, that in truth, in spite of the friendship which has always existed between us, I sometimes feel an instinctive terror when I see it."

"See, now!" exclaimed the old man, clapping his hands together as a child might have done.

"For my part," added Alma, "I always do what she wishes."

"You are a good child!" cried the old Count.

He took the girl's head between his hands, and kissed her two or three times on the hair, with deep emotion.

"Listen to me," he said. "If you are willing to oblige your old father, you can do so."

"I am quite ready. What is it, father?"

"Well, come every day, like today, and sit with me, that we may talk together for a few hours, as now. Your conversation is as charming as yourself, and you cannot believe how much it interests me, especially when you speak of that young girl, in whom, I don't know why, I feel so great an interest."

"With all my heart, father," replied Alma. "I am so fond of speaking of Regina, that it will be a very pleasant task to talk to you about her every day."

As she said this, she prepared to rise, but the old man detained her.

This conversation had warmed his heart as with sunlight; his eyes had lost their mournfulness, as he fixed them upon Alma's innocent face, endeavoring to evoke, by the aid of the descriptions which she had given him, the loved form of his daughter.

One cloud, however, still lingered on the old man's brow; one last doubt still weighed upon his heart.

He stretched out his hand to Alma, and made her sit close to him, has e said, with trembling accents:

"One word more. You know, doubtless, that the chief of the bandits, Andrea, is not her father?"

"I know it."

"And Regina, does she know it?"

"Yes, father."

"In your most intimate conversation, has she ever spoken as if she wished some day to see her relations— her own father?"

Alma reflected.

"Search your memory well, my child," added the old man.

And with eager eyes he endeavored to trace upon Alma's face the current of her thoughts.

"She has never spoken to me about it," was at length her answer.

The old man gave a long sigh, and his head, which had been for a moment erect, fell once more upon his breast. His forehead became deeply furrowed; a fold of bitter grief descended from the corners of his mouth, and he retired with trembling steps.

"Lean upon me, father!" said Alma.

"No!" he said, gently repulsing her. I now wish to be alone—alone! Leave me!"

Alma went back to her chamber, where her only resource against her melancholy and ennui was to summon Marina, whose gossip and pleasant ways succeeded for a time in making her forget her sorrows.

When he had reentered his rooms, Count Ercole threw himself into a chair, and buried his face in his hands.

"What can I do with this child?" he said. "Can I use her as an instrument of vengeance? No! She is so gentle, so good, and loves my child so. No! I could never bring myself to do that!"

He remained long in the same attitude, turning over a thousand projects in his brain, but unable to determine upon one.

When an hour had thus passed, he raised his head, drew his chair close to the desk, and wrote a letter which bore this direction: *To the Marquis of Santa Fiore, at his palace at Spoleto.*

The letter contained an invitation to a great hunting party, for the day after the morrow.

The letter was confided to a valet, who mounted his horse and set off at once.

At that moment, Alma dreamed of Mario,

PART TWO

I. The Boar Hunt

On the day appointed for the hunt, the castle wore a very unusual appearance. From the earliest dawn the courtyard was filled with people, and the music of trumpets awoke the ancient echoes of the fort.

The huntsmen were clothed in their finest uniforms; their horses richly harnessed, neighed with impatience in the midst of the court. The dogs, unaccustomed to such festivities, barked their loudest, and strained at their leashes.

The pack, or *valtratto*, which had been collected for the purpose of hunting wild boar, consisted of a number of hounds and a score of harriers, large and strong, and remarkable for the size of their heads and loins, their stalwart frames, and the fire in their eyes.

The crowd of men, horses, and dogs assembled on the award in front of the castle, under the shadow of the lofty trees, the crests of which the sun had now begun to gild, presented a spectacle that was infinitely festive.

Suddenly the trumpets sounded, "To horse! To horse!" and Count Ercole appeared, accompanied by the Marquis of Santa Fiore, who had arrived on the previous evening.

The Marquis was a gentleman of distinguished appearance. Although he was at least forty years of age, the pure and correct lines of his calm and noble countenance bore that expression of distinction and elegance, which is, even at the present day, to be observed amongst the descendents of the ancient Italians. His frame was well formed, and he sat on his horse in the style of an accomplished cavalier.

A richly ornamented litter followed the two gentlemen, and on its cushions reclined a young girl who appeared to take no interest in the activities. It was Alma. She yielded her exquisitely formed head to the undulations of the litter, her sad and pensive countenance rested on her shoulder. She glanced with indifferent eyes on the Marquis of Santa Fiore, and dreamed of Mario.

Mercedes, seated by Alma's side, counted her beads in the manner of Spanish duennas, who employ their rosaries similarly to how French women make use of their fans.

As for the Marquis of Santa Fiore, he inspected all the preparations with the utmost attention; for he took the greatest possible pleasure in hunting the wild boar, and displayed an ability in its pursuit which was universally acknowledged.

The gentlemen, full of curiosity, surrounded him closely, going into ecstasies at his pointed observations, and which displayed a long and well-versed experience. A circle had formed around him, and the Marquis seemed to enjoy all this admiration, even though he was accustomed to creating it. Everyone accepts renown wherever he may meet it.

At length the trumpet sounded the note of departure. The drawbridge was let down, and the company set forth.

"Signor, my host," said Santa Fiore to Count Ercole, "your dogs are too fat."

"I am an old man, my good Marquis," replied Ercole, "and overwhelmed with cares. It will depend on you whether or not these hounds shall be kept in fitter condition. You will do me the greatest honor and pleasure by coming to hunt with me often."

"I accept your invitation very heartily indeed, my dear Count," replied Santa Fiore, "for I confess to you that I am passionately fond of hunting wild boar, and my estates are by no means favorable for it. It is only by chance that my bloodhounds roust a half-grown one, and a full-grown one I have not seen for years."

During this conversation the cavalcade had descended into the valley of mingled wood and water, which we have already described several times. It had been many years since such an animated company had set out from Ercole Vitelli's castle. Everyone was in good humor, especially the gentlemen of the court, amongst whom our old acquaintances Pasquale Contarini, Capitan, and Tiberio Fanferluizzi, were prominent and made more noise than all the rest.

Pasquale, whose nose was as red and shining as the rising sun, gave long, frequent kisses to his flask, swearing by Bacchus that it was prudent, when on a hunting expedition, to fortify one's self against the morning air.

Tiberio Fanferluizzi, clothed in a magnificent hunting costume, declaimed a sonnet to Diana, who, as everyone knows, is the goddess of hunters.

Capitan recounted, although no one listened to him, how he had brought to bay and slain by himself, and without the aid of dogs, a boar of the largest proportions.

Such conversations, interspersed with lively repartee, gave an air of gaiety to the whole party.

In the meantime, the more it penetrated the depth of the valley, the road became more difficult. The blood-hounds, their necks straining at their leashes, scented the ground with the utmost eagerness. The horses neighed and champed at their bits.

The cavalcade rode through wild country, amidst the glorious sunshine of the morn. The air was fresh and balmy; a more favorable day for hunting could not have been chosen.

"I think, my host," said the Marquis of Santa Fiore, "that we have reached a proper place for the sport. It is time to send the bloodhounds on the track."

"I rely entirely on your skill," said the Count, who perceived with secret satisfaction the Marquis's animation. "Give your orders to the huntsmen."

The Marquis desired nothing better, and at once descending from his horse, soon found amongst the bushes and on the moist ground certain traces which attracted his earnest attention. Bending down with one knee upon the ground, he said to the huntsmen who surrounded him:

"See here, gentlemen, this is the footmark of a male. The toes are large, and the footmarks close together. If it had been a female, the footmarks would have been wider apart, and the sole and heel larger."

Farther on, the Marquis pointed out, in a range of thickets, which closed the glade as with a hedge, certain marks named *boutis*, by the aid of which a skillful hunter is capable of judging the exact length and size of the head or the boar by which they have been made.

The dogs were immediately uncoupled, and the bloodhound put upon the track. Then the whole troop proceeded to advance at a more rapid pace towards the forest. At first, they traversed a sort of glade, crowded with brush and thickets, and speedily arrived at the lofty trees, which were, so to speak, the advanced sentinels of the forest, that stretched away to the left, broken by ravines and hills, and full of shade, silence, and mystery. On the left, through a line of trees, could be perceived the blue waters of the wild marsh pools, and their melancholy shores.

The track of the wild boar appearing to lie in this direction, the troop of hunters hurried along it like a whirlwind, but speedily met with a disappointment; for the dogs, with eyes on fire, and hanging tongue, paused at the edge of the water.

"I will wager," cried the Marquis of Santa Fiore, "that we shall find the *souil* of a wild boar, and nothing more."

And he pointed with the end of his hunting-whip across the reeds, to a spot on the muddy ground on the edge of the pool, where there was the impression of the belly of a boar—which is termed, in the hunting phraseology of Italy, a *souil*. To judge by that *souil*, it was a boar of enormous size.

"Well, gentlemen," said the Marquis, "since we will not find him here, we must seek him in his den."

Thereupon the cavalcade set forth in quest of the boar in the direction of the forest. The bloodhound, a lone-tailed, courageous beast, rushed forward in advance, and the pack and the hunters hastened to follow him.

Suddenly the Marquis, who was the foremost of the latter, rose in his stirrups, and shouted out that cry so well-known to hunters:

"View, halloo, there!"

And at that moment, a black mass bounded into the thicket with surprising agility.

"View, halloo! View, halloo!" cried the Marquis, his eyes sparkling with animation.

The boar was flying, in fact, with the utmost precipitation towards the forest. Then all the hunters began to shout with all their might:

"See, dogs, see! Hoo, there! Hoo, hi! Ho, dogs, ho!"

The troop swept onwards towards the forest at a gallop, careless of all objects, and of the serious danger they might encounter.

Alma's litter, of course, could not follow, and the men who bore it were already out of breath. They attempted to proceed, but the obstacles so easily surmounted by horsemen, were almost insurmountable to men on foot, bearing a heavy burden.

Alma was by no means anxious to see a poor animal killed; and her heart was genuinely too good not to make her feel great compassion for the weary men who bore her litter; so she ordered them to set her down, and follow the hunt, if they pleased, until it was time to return to the castle.

The bearers did not need to hear this order twice; at once, they set down the litter—their curiosity being stronger than their fatigue—and hastened to rejoin the hunters.

Alma thus remained alone with Mercedes, on the edge of the forest, between its first trees and the marsh pools. Inspired by a feeling of antipathy which she could not explain to herself, she avoided the company of the duenna, and always founds reasons, sometimes on one pretext and sometimes on another, to avoid her. She did not attempt, therefore, to disturb her, as she sat at the foot of an oak, fingering her beads.

The yellow iris, the white water lily, and the myosotis, grew on the borders of the pool in the midst of many other superb and delicate flowers; some remarkable for their singular forms, and others for their curious perfumes, and all for that wild and lovely grace which distinguishes aquatic flora.

Alma felt her heart dilate at the sight of this rich and beauteous nature; and without thinking anymore of the hunt, which was now at some distance, she slowly wandered along the perfumed banks, thinking of those whom she had left behind.

As she went along, she plucked one by one, red, white, and purple flowers, which seemed almost to naturally group themselves into a lovely bouquet in her hand.

Alma was terribly sad. She had never cared for fortune or rank; she had been happy amidst the mountains where she had passed her childhood. What had seemed to be her lot—the simple and humble mode of life to which she had appeared destined—had been exactly suited to her tender and submissive character; and, for her, who had never dreamed of greater joy than to receive Mario's loving glance, it was sad to have to look forward to a perpetual association with the Marquis of Santa Fiore and Count Ercole.

Alma thought of all these things and sighed.

Suddenly, she heard a noise beside her, and, after few seconds' attention, perceived at two paces distant the glitter of two fiery eyes.

At first the young girl was frightened; but she readily overcame her first impulse of childish terror, and recognized the poor woman who had followed her in her exile, and who, two or three before, had waved kisses to her from the exterior bastion of the fort.

Seen thus amidst the flags and the water lilies, the poor beggar woman might have been taken for some spirit of the marsh.

Alma ran to her, but when the poor woman rose, radiant with joy and hope, her eyes suddenly encountered in the distance the pale and meager profile of Mercedes.

At the sight of the duenna, the Woman in grey trembled. An indefinable expression of terror spread over her features, and she staggered back, stretching out her arms.

"Oh, that woman, that woman!" she exclaimed, knitting her brows.

"You are trembling," said Alma.

"Let us not remain here," replied the Woman in grey. "I wish to speak with you, but the presence of that woman chills me with fear."

"I will follow you," said Alma.

Then the Woman in grey left the edge of the pool, and, gliding from thicket to thicket, as if she feared that Mercedes might see her, gained the wood, turning from time to time see whether Alma followed.

The young girl did so, smiling.

Without knowing why, Alma felt herself drawn by a sweet and irresistible sympathy towards this poor woman, who seemed to love her so much. In this, her exile, the Woman's was the only face she could look on without fear, her heart the only one into which she felt disposed to pour all that her own contained of bitterness and sadness.

So Alma followed her, smiling.

At every step they took, the voices of the hunters fell still more faintly on their ears, and they soon ceased to hear anything but the rustling of the leaves in the breeze, or the rich songs of the free and happy birds. The wood became more dense. There was, doubtless, no human habitation near, and for a young girl to venture so far alone, might very probably be dangerous.

But Alma thought nothing of all this. The poor woman called her and Alma followed her, smiling.

At length the Woman in grey paused, and Alma did the same. The spot which they had reached was a small alcove, some four feet square, into which the rays of the sun penetrated like a shower of gold. It was surrounded with lofty brushwood, mingled with tall trees. A tree rose from amidst the brushwood—a dwarf oak, whose gnarled trunk terminated, at about a men's height from the ground, by a knotted mass, from which escaped, like a luxuriant mass of hair, many vigorous branches.

At the foot of this tree a quantity of thick moss formed a soft and comfortable seat; the poor woman bade Alma sit down upon it, forcing her, with an air of tender authority, to lean against the tree.

Alma did as her companion wished, and seemed to take a pleasure in submitting to the poor woman's every desire.

The latter gazed at her a moment, with an expression of ineffable pleasure, as if she felt that now, for the first time, the young girl was in her possession, and that in that solitude no one could interfere with her happiness.

An idea, full of love and grace, entered her soul. She plucked a hemlock flower and a branch of ivy, and, weaving the delicate flower in the latter, made a wreath which she placed on Alma's beautiful locks.

Then she knelt down, and, contemplating her a moment with mute admiration, exclaimed, clasping her hands:

"Oh, you are beautiful!"

And, indeed. Alma did look charming. The hemlock, with its soft, rose-colored flowers, its pale and indented foliage mingled with the dark ivy with a wild gracefulness of effect, which gave to Alma's physiognomy an ideal and poetic character, with which the dullest imagination would have been struck.

Without knowing why, Alma was deeply moved by these testimonies of affection bestowed on her by the poor woman. The emotion she experienced embarrassed her, and she sought relief by breaking the silence:

"Is it long," she asked, slightly blushing, "since you have been in the mountain?"

"I have just come from it," replied the Woman. "I always wander now, and I go alternately from the mountain to the plain, and from the plain to the mountain. Oh! I pray God that He will maintain my strength."

"Poor woman" said Alma, with a voice full of compassion. "But what can compel you to wander thus about the country?"

"A fatality," replied the Woman in grey, a frown suddenly settling upon her forehead.

Alma felt a chill at her heart, and she was almost frightened; but the Woman had said that she had just come from the mountain, and curiosity gave her courage.

"And what did you see in the mountain?" she anxiously inquired. "Regina, doubtless, did you not? Ah! If she feels for me only little of the friendship I feel for her, she must have wept much since my departure."

"I have seen Regina," said the Woman in grey, shaking her head. "She was riding her little black horse along the mountain paths, and there was no trace of sorrow on her brow."

"Always restless," said Alma, while an amiable smile played upon her lips. "It is she who gives life and animation to the mountain, which would be a very dull abode without her. Regina is my uncle's joy; if she were ever to leave him, Andrea would die."

"Andrea has been very sad since your departure," interrupted the Woman in grey.

"Do you think so?"

"I have seen him."

"Poor uncle!"

"He stood upon the summit of the plateau which commands the valley; his head hung low, his arms were crossed upon his breast. It is said that he has changed much since your departure."

"Is it possible?"

"He is now extremely severe towards his men; everyone trembles at his approach."

"Poor uncle!" murmured Alma, though in a reverie.

The words of the poor woman carried her back to that period of her life when, free and happy, she had experienced the development and growth of the dearest sentiments of her heart. She bitterly recalled to mind those days, now gone forever, and, with the instinctive terror of a child, looked forward to the future which was in reserve for her, and which a dark veil now concealed.

At length she raised her head, and, looking gently at her companion, while a timid blush colored her cheeks, and her bosom heaved as if with difficulty, said:

"There is another person at the fort, whom I have not seen since my departure. Do you know what has become of my cousin Mario?"

"Oh! The sight of him is enough to make one's heart bleed!" replied the Woman in grey. "His sadness is indescribable; he wanders to fro perpetually, with languid steps and hanging head; he seems to return scarcely sufficient energy to carry his musket. Frequently he goes to sit by the little spring where you so often sat with him and where I saw you sometimes together. Poor child!

My reminding you of that saddens you, and makes you weep!"

And, indeed, tears which were at the same time both sweet and bitter, flowed down Alma's cheeks. The words of the poor woman had revealed to her Mario's love for her, and her heart was at the same time both sad and happy.

"You weep, my child?" continued the woman. "Oh! You must love him, then?"

"I?" said Alma, full of confusion.

"You love him!" repeated the Woman in grey, nodding her head. "Oh! I know it, my child. And why blush for a sentiment so pure, and which contains all your happiness and all your hopes. Love! Love without fear, for love comes from God, and is a noble and holy sentiment. Before they return from the chase, Alma, should you like to hear a charming story of love? It is a consolation to those who love, to hear recounted the sufferings of others…"

"A love story?" said Alma, smiling through her tears.

"Yes. A charming narrative, worthy of the old times of chivalry, although the incidents it recounts took place only a few years since."

"Oh, yes! I should like to hear it!" said Alma. "Sit close to me. The sun not yet in the middle of the sky; we have plenty of time before us."

The Woman in grey scarcely awaited this invitation, but at once sat down at Alma's feet and thus began.

II. A Love Story

"May it please God, my dear girl," the Woman in grey began, "that you may never suffer such miseries as it seemed good to providence to inflict on the heroine of my story. She was not as you are, beautiful and pure; she had none of the charming qualities which attract all eyes and hearts towards you; but she was good and gentle as you are, and like you, my child, she had within her the divine germ of all the virtues.

"At fifteen years of age she was alone, without the protection of relatives, and lost in the midst of a world of which she knew nothing. At sixteen years she became the mistress of a great lord; a year, a single year, sufficed to consummate her dishonor, and to give to her name a humiliating celebrity."

"And what was her name?" asked Alma, with interest.

"Her name is long forgotten," replied the Woman in grey, "although it was once so famous that you may possibly have heard it in your childhood. She was named Lucrezia Mammone."

The Woman in grey pronounced this name in such bitter a tone that it did not escape Alma's attention. But the latter searched her memory in vain, and, shaking her pretty head, replied, with a gentle glance at her companion:

"I do not know that name."

"You were too young to know it."

"Well, it does not matter," said Alma, "pray continue."

"Lucrezia," continued the woman, "had never really known what love was. Love is a celestial sentiment which can only take root in a pure heart, and Lucrezia, up to a certain time, had left her heart open to all the dissoluteness of a courtesan's life. She was not, however, an utterly lost creature, and the existence which she led had not entirely corrupted her!

"One day, amongst the young gentlemen who surrounded her, and paid her assiduous court, she particularly noticed one named Angelo. He had not approached her with that insolent familiarity of manner which is often assumed by great gentlemen towards the poor creatures whom misfortune has thrown into an evil course of life. When in her presence he never passed the bounds of the most complete reserve, and displayed towards her the politeness and respect he would have accorded his wife or his sister.

"To say at what particular moment the poor creature was touched by this conduct would be impossible. There was, in Angelo's tender and respectful bearing, so much reverence and chaste affection, that Lucrezia felt as if it regenerated her, and under the inspiration of this new sentiment, her heart began to dream of a new existence. Angelo loved her and she loved him. At length she knew the joys of a pure love, and this love would have doubtless saved her from infamy, if a great catastrophe had not occurred to crush her.

"One day, just before sunset, a stranger entered Lucretia's house and said:

" 'I am your brother.'

"This man was an adventurer beyond the pale of the law; a man, however, with a large heart, and a spirit as finely tempered as steel. He revealed to the lost Lucrezia a secret—a terrible secret—that of her birth. Lucrezia—

that unhappy creature of infamous name—belonged to one of the noblest families of Italy. Alas! it was too late to begin life anew; and when Lucrezia demanded of him, whilst she trembled:

" 'My brother! Shall I live or die?'

"Her brother gave no answer. He wept, but his heart remained immoveable, and he did not utter single word of regret or grief.

"Then Lucrezia Mammone, sobbing, embraced him, bade him one last adieu, and, recommending to his care a poor infant she had brought into the world during her dissolute life, fled, without daring to look back. At the end of the garden in which this conversation had taken place ran a river. Lucrezia gave one thought to her child. another to God, and then threw herself into the water, which closed above her head."

"Poor woman!" said Alma, sighing deeply.

"Ah! Was it not sad indeed!" replied the Woman in grey, who seemed comforted by this compassionate expression, called forth by her recital. "Was it not hard thus to quit life at seventeen years, just at the moment when a pure and chaste love had begun to purify it?"

"It is a sad story!" murmured the young girl.

"Oh! But it is not yet finished," said the strange woman.

"She did not die, then?"

"Someone saved her!"

"Angelo! I will wager!"

"Yes, Angelo!"

"I thought so!" cried Alma, clapping her little hands together in naive and gentle pleasure.

The Woman in grey smiled, and that smile gave to her pale countenance a momentary but infinite charm. She took Alma's hands and kissed them.

"Yes," she said, "it was he! He carried her to the shore and recalled her to life. When Lucrezia recovered her senses, she perceived at her feet—his hands joined in an attitude of prayer to God—the pale countenance of him whom she loved.

" 'You wished to die, then?' said Angelo, with a gentle air of reproach.

" 'It was necessary,' replied Lucrezia.

" 'But to die without me?' continued Angelo. 'Do you not love me, then?'

"Lucrezia burst into tears. She had neither strength nor courage left. The tortures she had experienced were still present in her memory. They had not overthrown her reason ; but the slightest shock, the least remembrance of the past, sent a shiver through all her nerves, and caused convulsive trembling of her limbs.

"A terrible fear took possession of her. She trembled lest she should encounter her brother, that man who, for the honor of a great name had, in a certain manner, commanded her to die. She had been too near to death not to tremble at the thought her brother might order her a second time to quit this world.

"Angelo took her, therefore, to an inn outside of town."

"What was the name of the town?" interrupted Alma.

"Spoleto," replied the poor woman. "Angelo was ignorant of the motives which had led to this suicide attempt; but he did not wish to appear indiscreet at such a moment. He had a chamber prepared for Lucrezia, and another for himself; for he was unwilling to lose sight of this woman, whom he loved with all his soul, and whom he had miraculously snatched from death.

"On the following day, at dawn, his first care was to inquire about Lucrezia; but when he sent the hostess to her chamber, it was found to be empty. Lucrezia had departed more than two hours earlier.

"Angelo was in despair. He made diligent inquiries, and found that Lucrezia had taken the road leading to Rome. He scattered his money with open hand, and traversed all the chief roads; but it was in vain. He searched for her all over Italy for many months; but she had concealed herself with a care which blocked all his efforts.

"At last, he found her in Naples, in a house in the Rue de Toledo.

" 'Oh! Now,' he cried, 'I will never quit you more!'

" 'Pardon me, Angelo!' she said, giving him her hand. 'I did not wish to associate my lost life with yours. It is a great misfortune that you have found me; it is a still greater misfortune that you did not let me die. But I no longer have fortitude enough to leave you.'

"From that day, they lived together under the same roof as brother and sister. It then that Lucrezia tasted the only moments of happiness she had ever had—a happiness which at the best was sad and austere, and which lasted but a short time.

"In her turn she followed Angelo. The latter had a command in the Spanish army; and the chances of war carried him from Naples to the south of Italy. Lucrezia followed him across the Basilicata and Calabria.

"It was a rude sort of life which she now led, and one that was continually mingled with ever-growing fear. Lucrezia bore every fatigue with heroic courage, which was due only to her love for Angelo.

"Each week, however, witnessed a fresh engagement; and it was impossible to say when Italy would again enjoy peace.

"Moreover, Angelo was exposed to serious dangers; and fortune, which had hitherto been so favorable to him, might very easily turn against him. And, at length, it did.

"One day Angelo was brought to her, pale, covered with blood, deeply wounded in the breast.

"In the midst of the hazards of adventurous life which he led, it had never occurred to Lucrezia that her Angelo might be wounded; it had never occurred to her that he might die.

"He was the only link that chained her to life, her only happiness, her only joy. How was it possible for her to believe that God would deprive her of this one consolation?

"When Angelo was laid upon his bed of suffering, she would permit no one to approach or tend him but herself. During three months she watched night and day by his pillow. She had entered upon one of those desperate struggles with death, in which the combatant must either be victorious or perish. Love and death had a hand-to-hand struggle, and love proved the stronger."

"Oh, how glad I am!" cried Alma, joyously.

"No! Do not rejoice too soon!"

"What happened, then?" exclaimed the young girl.

"Angelo's wound closed; but he did not regain his strength. He walked with trembling steps, like an old man; and after a time, he could not even go round his chamber resting on Lucrezia's arm. Soon he had to take to his bed again; and day by day the unhappy woman saw life slowly fading away from the man whom she loved more than anything.

"Angelo said nothing, but he felt that he was dying, and from time to time his eyes fixed themselves with strange tenacity upon Lucrezia. One might said that, understanding that he was about to leave her forever, he wished to carry away with him her image, at least, to the other world.

"Lucrezia had the inexpressible grief of seeing that youthful and energetic spirit grow weaker day by day; and when, my child, you shall have had experience of life, and shall know what a pure love is to a poor degraded creature who hopes, by means of this love, to attain her redemption, then you will understand what this unhappy woman suffered.

"Angelo, living under the same roof as her, and loving her with all his soul, treated her with as much respect as if she had been in the midst of the most respectable of families. The two scarcely ventured even to shake hands. Lucrezia had so much need of respect, that she could not venture to grant that which the purest young girl may accord to her betrothed; and Angelo, comprehending this holy timidity, behaved towards her with as much respect as he would have shown towards a chaste child.

"The end, however, of this long agony was near at hand.

"One evening, Lucrezia, by the vacillating light of a half-extinguished lamp, knelt behind a curtain and, with clasped hands, prayed for the dying man.

"When her prayer was ended, she arose and approached the bed. The prayer had suddenly calmed her fears and allayed her terrible apprehensions; but, when she reached the couch and saw her lover lying pale and motionless, a sudden terror took possession of her, an icy chill passed beneath her hair, and she uttered a stifled cry.

"It seemed to her that Angelo had neither breath nor sight!

"She ran wildly to the lamp, and, seizing it with a trembling hand, returned with haggard eyes to hold it near Angelo.

"In the meantime the latter had not stirred.

"She placed her hand upon his lips; he breathed no longer!

"She touched his heart; it beat no longer!

"She called him over and over by his name, and he made no answer!

"Then, without uttering a cry, without a single groan, she fell upon her knees by her lover, and prayed; and then, as if she had suddenly drawn from her despair the strength and energy which had hitherto been wanting in her, she rose with a certain solemnity and then she leaned over the bed, trembling like a virgin at the entrance of the nuptial chamber.

" 'Oh, Angelo!' she said with a grave voice. 'While you lived, a kiss from my mouth never touched your lips; but death unites what life kept apart; and now, O Angelo, my betrothed, my spouse! Receive the supreme kiss; and may God bless our union!'

"Speaking thus, she leaned over the corpse and joined her lips to the pale and cold lips of Angelo. It was her first night of love!"

When the Woman in grey had concluded, she gazed at Alma, who sobbed.

"Dear Alma!" She said, smiling through her tears. "Thank you for your compassion. Believe me, Lucrezia deserved it."

"And what became of her?" asked the young girl, wiping away her tears.

"Angelo lies in a small cemetery in Calabria, beneath a rose-laurel, on slope facing the sea."

"And Lucrezia?"

"Oh! Lucrezia's story is still sad one. After the poor woman had lost her lover, she remembered that she still had a child, and returned to the region she had left for the purpose of following Angelo. She wandered from town to town, returning every year to weep on Angelo's tomb; and frequently she even approached Spoleto and traversed the Abruzzi; but her dread of her brother always prevented her from remaining long nearby, although her maternal instinct, which had become strong in her heart, drew her thither incessantly."

"Oh! Why did I not know this woman?" cried Alma. "I would have wept with her; for she has been so unhappy, and I feel that I should have loved her!"

The Woman in grey listened to Alma's words with a delight impossible to describe. Her lips were parted, and she stretched out her arms to the young girl.

As Alma uttered the last word, she fell at her feet and embraced her knees.

"Love me, then, celestial angel," she exclaimed, with all the vehement passion of love, "for I am Lucrezia!"

"Poor woman!" murmured the young girl, pressing her to her heart.

They remained for a moment in a close embrace, weeping, and unable to speak.

"But you had a daughter?" asked Alma, gently withdrawing herself from the poor woman's arms.

"Oh, yes! A gentle, charming child, who would be your age today. But where is she now? And will my heart recognize her when I meet her? Oh! May God enlighten me, so that I may not deceive myself."

"Have you seen her?"

"Yes."

"Long ago?"

"Since some weeks only."

"Ah, well," said Alma, with a charming gesture, "then you will bring her to me, will you not? I should like so to see her; and if you have confidence in me, if you really love me, you will leave her at the castle. I am alone there, and all is dull. She will be more to me than a companion. It is so long that I have wished for a sister."

Lucrezia, trembling with emotion, listened to her words without replying; but Alma was about to continue, there was suddenly heard a great clamor of horses, and dogs, and horns.

"The hunt!" cried Lucrezia, afraid.

She threw at the same moment upon Alma a glance full of sadness and regret; and as the noise approached nearer and nearer, she fled, concealing herself behind one thicket after another.

Alma rose in her turn, and regained the margin of the pool, where she found Mercedes, who had been anxiously seeking her. At the same moment the hunt issued from the wood.

The voice of the Marquis was heard far off, shouting:

"Hou vori!"

Which means that the boar is turning. And, in fact, the boar suddenly rushed from the brush, with flaming eyes, bristles erect, grunting terribly.

He making for the water; but the dogs intercepted him. The pack passed, eager and furious, with hanging tongues, and eyes filled with blood.

Four old hounds, whose necks were protected by collars, leaped upon the boar's flanks, attacking him with the utmost courage, and avoiding his blows with great skill.

The horsemen sallied from the wood with the Marquis of Santa Fiore at their head.

"Let loose a couple of harriers," he cried. "It is time to dress the boar's head."

One of the huntsmen who held the dogs in leash released a couple of the strongest, who, with a single bound, threw themselves upon the boar's head, and seized him by the ears. This is what is meant by "dressing the boar's head." The animal thus seized could no longer flee.

The Marquis of Santa Fiore immediately leaped from his horse, and, drawing a short hunting sword which he had by his side, approached the boar.

He seized hold of the beast's hair, and then, resting the blade upon his left hand, so as to conduct it and keep it firm, and not wound the dogs, he pierced the beast at four fingers' lengths beneath the shoulder. The animal fell stone dead.

It was, indisputably, an exploit worthy of the best hunter of the region, and all the members of the hunt applauded him vehemently.

The Marquis of Santa Fiore bad executed the difficult operation with remarkable coolness and the most perfect elegance.

Alma turned her face any from this scene of bloodshed, and rejoined her litter.

The cavalcade drew up in order, after having placed the boar upon the branches of a tree, arranged in the form of a hand-barrow, and regained the castle, accompanied by the blowing of horns and the songs of the huntsmen.

A splendid repast awaited the Prince's guests, and every one ate and drank as people do when they are in good health, and have passed the day in hunting.

At dessert, however, the old Count, who had not lost sight of the object which had led him to invite the Marquis, turned the conversation to the subject of marriage. Pressed by his host, the Marquis declared that he had for some time been thinking of getting married, as he wished an heir, and that he cared neither for fortune nor love with his wife, provided the girl were handsome, virtuous, and of high birth.

Ercole hinted that he would be proud to have a man like the Marquis for a son-in-law; whilst the latter replied that he thought that Alma to be very charming. It will thus be seen that the matter was in good trim, and that the success of Prince Ercole's project seemed certain.

Till far into the night the company swallowed the fine wines from the cellars of the castle.

III. Bel Demonio

As Prince Ercole and the Marquis of Santa Fiore emptied their wine cups and talked about marriage, it became night.

Neither moon nor stars were visible in the heavens. A funereal darkness covered the whole sky, and extended over the valley like the dome of a sepulcher.

It was a deep, black night, sinister as that in which Macbeth had assassinated his guest, the king, and his two grooms.

The sentinels upon the bastions kept watch, leaning on their muskets. And, in the midst of the solemn silence, nothing was heard but the monotonous *Who goes there?* which they uttered from time to time.

At the castle, apart from the sounds of the hunting party, who, from time to time, made themselves heard, all was profoundly still. The soldiers and grooms had surrendered themselves to the pleasures of repose. The dogs and the under huntsmen, weak from fatigue, endeavored to repair, as they might, the strength which they had lost during the day. But it was amidst the mountains especially, that the night took on an aspect full of sadness and horror.

From the depths of the stupendous gorges could be heard the howling of the ferocious wolves of the Apennines, whose hoarse voices mingled with the roar of the torrents.

The bittern whistled in the marshes, and fled with fright when some hunting fox passed by.

In the air, evil-foreboding clouds of screech owls whirled; and the wind, mingling its grand, sad voice with this concert of strange cries, swept up the valley, carrying with it the dust of the road and the withered leaves of the forest.

It was a terrible night to be a wandering traveler.

But there are men so strong-willed in their nature that they fear neither wounds nor death; neither the teeth of the wolf nor the dagger of the brigand.

At two leagues from the plateau on which stood the camp of the free companies, commanded by Andrea Vitelli, at the summit of the most inaccessible mountains, was a mysterious villa; a villa which had an ominous aspect, which would have inclined an observer to have taken it more for a mausoleum than a human habitation. For its gates and windows were always closed, and it looked as if death had recently passed by, or that the proprietor did not venture to inhabit it. There are indeed properties which time and circumstances render uninhabitable.

That of which we speak surely looked uninhabited, that is to say, it looked as if it as haunted only by bats and evil spirits.

In a country as superstitious as Italy, the latter belief was not without value, as it alone had sufficed to protect the villa far better than a troop of regular soldiers could have.

Honest people and bandits have, in fact, one thing in common—they fear the Devil more than God!

During this night, the dim, mute outline of the villa stood out against the black background of the sky. As usual, its doors and windows were hermetically closed; and it had, on this occasion, an particularly fatal and somber aspect.

No light was visible from the interior.

The villa seemed plunged into the most complete abandonment, and had around it only a few firs, which stood as motionless as those frail and scanty shrubs which are planted around tombs.

Suddenly...

Ah! If Cocomero, or some other peasant of the valley, or some brave knight, such as Signor Capitan, or some man without faith, law, fear, or conscience, such as Cosimo, or any other bravo of Andrea's band, had passed by at that moment, he would have staggered back and hastened to make the sign of the cross. But neither Cocomero, nor Cosimo, nor even the valiant Capitan, were passing at that hour, and no obstacle was there to prevent what was about to take place.

Suddenly, one of the windows on the first story of the mysterious villa opened, like an eye that wakes, and, in the space formed by the open window, a black head, wearing an Asiatic turban, stretched out with an air of inquiry.

When the owner of the black head had glanced around the silent and deserted plain, it was slowly withdrawn, and the window was once more closed.

A moment afterwards the gate of the villa grated on its hinges; a young horseman, clothed in black, wearing a velvet mask, and mounted on a small Arab steed, sprang forth, prancing and caracoling.

Twelve horsemen followed him, twelve black horsemen, whose heads were encircled with large turbans, and who were armed with long damascened scimitars.

These twelve horsemen were not born on the southern coast of Africa; they were handsome, tall, supple, and robust, and rode their fiery horses with an address and skill which was almost miraculous.

As soon as the young man saw them at his side, he made a proud motion with his head, which was partly child-like and partly feminine, and, pointing to the plain which stretched out before them, struck his spurs into the sides of his little steed, and set off at a gallop.

The twelve horsemen followed him, and the gate closed behind them, without the aid of any human hand, as if it had obeyed some invisible impulse.

The little troop passed like the wind along the narrow steep paths of the mountain.

The twelve horsemen did not utter a word. The manes of their horses streamed along with the air, and their long white burnouses floated around them like pale clouds.

Their horses seemed not so much to gallop as to fly; in spite of the profound darkness of the night, and the complete absence of any visible road, in spite of the rocks and the quagmires, they moved like the wind.

"Forward! Forward!" from time to time cried the young chief.

And at the sound of his voice the horses and horsemen seemed to renew their energy, as if animated by some superhuman ardor. They crossed ravines and mountains, thickets and forests, marshes and torrents.

Whither were they going thus, in the midst of the night, silent as specters, and rapid as the genii of another world?

On what mysterious errand were they thus wildly rushing? What strange purpose moved them? To what conflict were they hurrying?

The twelve horsemen maintained the most profound and above the regular tramp of the thirteen horses could occasionally be heard the high and delicate voice of the young chief, urging them:

"Onward!"

As they penetrated farther and farther into the deepest gorges, the wolves, attracted by the scent of the horses, hurried after them in hot pursuit; but the horsemen still pressed ever onwards and, in proportion, as they crossed fresh ravines, other wolves joined the first, and performed the Devil's own dance amongst them.

By-and-by the wolves formed an enormous band, famished and terrible. Their eyes sparkled in the darkness, their tongues hung quivering from their lips, their bristling tails lashed their rough flanks, and they rent the air with exultant howls, as if they were certain of their prey.

The twelve horsemen, however, seemed not the least worried by this, and their chief, his locks floating on the moist night air, continued to lead them, and to repeat, in his high- pitched voice:

"Forward! Forward!"

But when one wolf, bolder than his fellows, sprang forward to seize his horse by the nostrils, he rapidly drew his scimitar, and with a supple, vigorous arm struck off the animal's hideous head.

And thus did each horseman, when it was necessary to defend his steed.

Speedily rocks, torrents, fir trees, marshes, and ravines disappeared, and the hooves of the horses touched the plain.

The wolves, pausing at the last outcroppings of the mountains, accompanied the cavalcade still with their prolonged howls.

Then, after a time, nothing was heard but the thunder of the horses on the sonorous ground, and the voice of the young chief.

At length the troop arrived beneath the walls of the castle of Count Ercole. Then the young chief slackened the speed of his horse, and made it perform, on the very brink of the moat, caracoles which the boldest rough rider would scarcely have ventured in broad daylight.

At that moment Alma entered her chamber and leaned upon her window sill. Perhaps she thought of the poor woman who had related to her the love story, perhaps of Mario. But, for whatever reason, her soul was still full of emotion, and open to the gentle impressions which had been produced by Lucrezia Mammone's story.

Lucrezia had related to her a story of love, and this story had enlightened her as to that which was passing in her own heart.

She loved Mario, she loved him with all the wild abandonment of a first love; and now—now they were separated, separated forever!

Alma closed her eyes, and pressed her hand to her heart, which beat violently.

When she raised her head, she saw in the distance, in the shadows, the twelve horsemen with their white mantles, passing upon the mound against the castle.

At first, she believed that she was the victim to some nocturnal hallucination; but she had experienced phantoms which existed only in her imagination, and these usually disappeared as suddenly as they had come. These horsemen, however, remained stationary around their young chief, and already a certain degree of agitation prevailed through the castle.

"Holy Virgin! What is about to happen?" cried Alma seized with an indescribable feeling of terror.

She immediately blew out her light, and crouched beneath the curtains.

The sentinel on the bastion had seen the small troop pass by; but instead of raising his musket to his shoulder and crying "*Who Goes There?*" he had let the butt end of his weapon fall heavily to the earth, made the sign of the Cross, invoking his patron saint, and murmuring:

"Bel Demonio!"

"Forward!" cried the young chief, with a laughing voice.

The horses extended their limbs and their necks, and once more swept over the ground.

Soon the horsemen saw the white walls and glittering lamps of a whole town appear amidst the thick shadows of the night. The clock tower stood out against the sky, and in the midst of the silence, arose confused murmurs—the noise of a city taking its pleasure.

It was Spoleto.

The horsemen drew up at the entrance of the town, under the porch of an isolated house, and suddenly disappeared.

Half an hour later, a sumptuous litter, carried by four men, issued from the house, and was borne in the direction of the theater of Spoleto.

As it was borne along, the crowd drew aside with a show of admiration and everyone said aloud:

"Make way for Countess Orsini!"

This name produced upon the populace in the streets of Spoleto an effect that was truly magical; and when the door of the litter opened, a great crowd of gentlemen surrounded it, bending with all reverence before the young lady who issued from it, clothed with royal magnificence.

The young Countess received, with charming grace, the homage which was paid to her, and reached her box escorted by murmurs of admiration. It appeared, however, that she was accustomed to such demonstrations, for, with the exception of certain formal greetings, which she exchanged with certain gentlemen, it was evident that the glorious reception with which she had met gave her but very slight satisfaction.

It was clearly manifest that she did not need to be told that she was beautiful, to know it.

Countess Orsini was, in fact, remarkably beautiful; her black and silken locks fell in profusion upon her round shoulders, which were as white as marble; she had a keen, clear eye, full of lights as bright as diamonds; and the saffron light of the chandeliers, falling upon her slightly bronzed cheeks, gave to her expression an animation and a brilliance which revealed, somewhat indirectly, perhaps, the voluptuousness of her person.

Countess Orsini was scarcely seventeen years of age, and yet she went into public alone. It was not known whether she had a mother, a husband, or a relation of any sort, and yet no one had ever been tempted to take advantage of this isolation, real or apparent; for it was quite evident that she possessed a firmness of character which would be sufficient to keep her admirers within the strictest bounds of respectful admiration.

In conversation, the Countess was at the same time sarcastic, epigrammatic, and imaginative; dry expressions of gallantry, in bad taste, would have had but little success in her presence. She had always ready upon her lips those barbed words which so pitilessly pierce the vain and the impertinent.

This satirical power was, to the Countess, more than equivalent to a venerable chaperon, a jealous husband, or a brother with heavy moustache.

On her first appearance at Spoleto, some young gentlemen had ventured to flood her box with bouquets and billets, but not one of them had ventured to boast that his offering had met with a particularly welcome reception. Some piquant remarks had issued from the Countess's pretty mouth on the subject; but the gallant gentle men who evidently appeared to be the subject of them, declared upon their honor that they were not addressed to them.

Countess Orsini's powers of sarcasm were, in fact, sufficient to keep at a distance every species of impertinence, and henceforth she was able to frequent the circles of society in Spoleto with as much security as if she had been escorted by a whole family of English Methodists.

In spite of her extreme youth, and the mute homage with which she was surrounded, the heart of Countess Orsini seemed untouched. She had not as yet shown signs of preference for any of the brilliant youths of Spoleto, and her conduct had not afforded grounds for the slightest suspicion. In fact, no one knew anything of her private life. She never paid visits, and never received any visitors at home; her servants never left her mansion, which was on the outskirts of the town. Her porters were as silent as the tomb; and although persons frequently took them to taverns to make them drunk on the best wine of the region, they never uttered a word. These good people were, indeed, secured against any temptation of that sort, by having had their tongues cut out.

The dowagers of Spoleto were, consequently, compelled to have recourse to the most fanciful suppositions. But the utmost fertility of imagination possessed by these good ladies did nothing to lead them to the truth; for the so-called Countess Orsini was, in fact, no other than the supposed niece of Andrea Vitelli—Regina.

For two years she had come thus, alone, and without the knowledge of Andrea or any of the person in the fort, to enjoy the *fêtes* and spectacles of Spoleto.

Sometimes, a young cavalier, wearing a mask accompanied her, and went back with her to the fort, but he never appeared at the theater nor any public place. The part he played was simply that of a complaisant brother, who obeyed the caprices of a too well-loved sister.

As Regina entered the theater, the first act was about to conclude. In all the boxes, conversation was being carried on with great earnestness, and in all the subject was the same.

Everyone was talking about the mysterious Bel Demonio, that fantastic brigand who overran the region, burned the castles of Prince Ercole, and devastated his domains, without anyone being able to explain the motive of his hatred against him, to say what he was really like, or to guess the place of his retreat.

But it was especially in Regina's box that the most extraordinary things were said about this mysterious personage.

"What is the news at Spoleto?" asked the young woman.

And the answer was that Bel Demonio had reappeared in the neighborhood, that he had been seen, that he was six feet tall, that he wore a long beard, and that his eyes, like a demon's, gave forth flames.

Regina laughed at these terrible stories, and declared that she was exceedingly anxious to see this Bel Demonio, of whom everyone spoke, but whom nobody could positively declare that he had seen.

And it was really marvelous with what infinite grace, and with what charming appearance of carelessness, she spoke of these things, without allowing the least trace of emotion to appear upon her countenance.

The young girl only desired to obtain these triumphs at Spoleto—to be considered beautiful, and to frighten all the young people and old women with the name of Bel Demonio!

When the performance was at an end, Regina, resuming her place in her litter, was conveyed towards the suburb of Spoleto; and the litter and its bearers speedily disappeared beneath the porch from which they had issued.

When the hour of one in the morning sounded from the clock tower of the town, the young masked cavalier, followed by his twelve Moors in their white mantles, issued from the house in the suburb.

"Forward!" cried the child-like voice.

And the whole troop, setting forth at a gallop, swept at the top of their speed over the plain, and disappeared like a whirlwind amidst the gorges of the mountains.

It was Regina! Bel Demonio, the terrible bandit, who burned the castles of old Prince Ercole, who continued to so desperately pursue the work of destruction commenced by Andrea, who filled the whole province with terror, was Regina.

Regina, the sister of Alma; Regina, in love with Mario! What had taken place in the heart of this girl, that she should have become one of Prince Ercole's most formidable adversaries? What fatal influence had drawn her into this mysterious mode of life! What inexplicable feeling had retained her in it, in spite of the strangeness of such a position for young woman?

Regina possessed one of those energetic beings who are frequently met in Italy; equally adapted for every mode of life, and constantly seeking, with desperate resolution, the complete satisfaction of those cravings with which nature has filled their hearts.

Reports had frequently been carried into the fortress commanded by Andrea of the splendid *fêtes* given by the Italian nobility at Spoleto. These accounts were filled with descriptions of balls, of theatrical performances, of handsome cavaliers with sparkling black eyes, of women with magnificent shoulders, and, without knowing why, Regina had felt her heart beat quicker as she listened to them.

Such accounts as these were so intoxicating for the imagination of a girl of seventeen years! A wild desire to participate in the doings of which she had thus heard took possession of her; and, one evening, leaning on Mario's arm, she had set out towards Spoleto.

On that first evening she had not, it is true, gone as far as Spoleto, but had stopped at a few hundred paces from the town, and there, in the midst of the calm and harmonious silence, had listened and had gazed.

She had listened to the confused murmurs of the *fêtes*, which the breeze had borne towards her; she had seen the thousand lights which sparkled in the darkness; and she had imagined what was going on behind the transparent veil of night.

Her heart beat in her young breast; cries of admiration, of eager desire, of enthusiastic delight, rushed from her quivering lips, and she had allowed Mario to become acquainted with her secret.

She wished to see more closely, to hear, to touch, all these marvelous realities which a veil of envy still concealed from her.

And then, Regina loved Mario, and Mario had not at that time any reason to refuse to her the satisfaction of the least of her caprices.

So Regina vent to Spoleto.

She drank with a sort of feverish intoxication of the cup of pleasure of this frivolous world; she drank long draughts of that empoisoned liquor which flattery pours into the hearts of young girls; she forgot everything for the moment, but to abandon herself—eager and almost mad—to that overwhelming whirlpool of desire which carried her towards unknown joys.

That which especially pleased Regina, however, it must be observed, was not so much the actual pleasures which she sought in the princely mansions of Spoleto; not so much that she heard herself on every side called beautiful, and could perceive her beauty reflected, so to speak, in the jealous glances of other women; it was not so much this which pleased her, as the journey, so rapid one way and so slow and pensive the other, which she often made to Spoleto in the company of Mario.

What pleased her best of all was the return. While the last notes of the harmonious concerts still lingered in her enchanted ears, while her heart still beat with the emotions with which it had been filled by the ball, Regina was glad to find herself alone with her cousin, in the midst of the silent plain—alone with him, and her thoughts and her throbbing heart.

Slightly veiled, the moon gently ascended the firmament; all was calm and silent, save that here and there might be heard the isolated cry of some nocturnal bird, or the harmoniously monotonous murmur of some neighboring rivulet.

Regina and Mario frequently rode along at a walking pace, without saying a single word, pensive, and filled with emotion.

Regina dreamed of all sort of thing; of the ball, of the night, and, most strongly, of Mario.

Mario thought of Andrea's fortress, of those who inhabited it, and, most strongly, of Alma.

It was strange; but always, after having enjoyed during some hours the splendid scenes she had so much desired to witness, Regina felt that something was still wanting in her, and that her life was as vapid and monotonous as before.

Long, long, she searched for the cause of this, and at length, she discovered it.

One evening she was returning from Spoleto. She had been riding a good hour side by side with Mario, and no word had passed between them.

The eyes of the young girl had ceased to gaze upon the indistinct outline of the plain, which was vaguely visible by the pale light of the moon.

Her breast heaved with sincere emotion. And this emotion was inspired—not by the remembrance of the ball she had just left; not by the praise she had received at it; not by the dreamy and poetic prospect spread out at that moment before her eyes—but by the handsome and melancholy features of her companion.

Of Mario! Her constant thought by day, her constant dream by night!

Of Mario, the young, the ardent, the enthusiastic, whose countenance during the last few months had assumed a certain dreamy expression, which added yet more to his serious and almost sad beauty.

Of Mario, whose mere glance filled her heart with emotion, and the sound of whose voice caused her breast to heave with the most singular feelings.

Regina slackened the pace of her horse, and drew nearer to her cousin, and then, leaning towards him with a gentle gesture which revealed all the loving disquiet of her heart, said, with a voice trembling with a thousand varied emotions:

"Mario! You are pensive this evening."

"I?" suddenly replied Mario, as if he had been abruptly roused from a dream, and giving Regina a look of astonishment.

"Yes; you are pensive," continued the young girl. "And I do not know the cause of your sadness. You have not confided in me, Mario, and that is bad of you."

Mario made a negative sign with his head, accompanied with a gesture of dreamy insolence.

"I do not lack confidence in you, Regina," he said, recovering his coolness and self-possession, "but at certain times, even as just now, I allow myself to be carried away by sweet reveries which make me forget that I am not alone. But be quite certain, my cousin, that there is no secret in my heart which I have any reason to conceal, and that I have no cause to distrust you."

Regina smiled somewhat bitterly, and stopped her horse, as she replied:

"Allow me, good cousin, to disbelieve every word you have just said. This is not the first time that I have had occasion to notice your taciturnity, and I must say that it hurts me. But, after all," she said, setting her horse in motion again, "it is no particular business of mine; and you are free, my cousin, to dream to your heart's content."

As she said this, she struck her spurs into Fuoco's sides, and rode rapidly in advance of her companion.

But, although the subject had, on this occasion, been dropped, Regina would not consider that she was beaten; and the importance, as it appeared to her, of knowing Mario's secret, induced her to employ her utmost skill in its discovery.

Regina loved Mario with that vehemence of feeling which she carried into everything she undertook.

Until now, it had never occurred to her that Mario might love some woman other than herself. She had thought that his military duties in Andrea's fortress would at least have prevented any affection for another from developing itself in his heart.

Her cousin's manner towards her, however, during the last few months, had caused her serious disquiet.

What was the cause of this sadness and taciturnity? She could not think of any subject which would be likely thus to preoccupy Mario's thoughts, and sought in vain to discover what had caused this change in his manner.

One moment, she believed that she herself was the cause of it, and that belief was sweet; but Mario behaved towards her only as usual, and nothing in his conduct showed that he was suffering from chagrin or jealousy.

Regina began to be seriously terrified; and, as she always pursued anything she undertook right to the end, she resolved to tear away the veil of mystery with her own hands, and to press Mario so closely on the subject, that he would be compelled to make a frank and open confession.

"Mario," she said one evening to her cousin, a moment before entering the fortress, "for some days, I have wanted to speak to you, and I am glad to have found this opportunity."

Mario had stopped upon being thus abruptly addressed, and although he did not know precisely what feelings agitated Regina's heart, a sudden suspicion of them flashed through his brain.

"Can you speak frankly?" continued Regina, in a firm voice, which betrayed no sign of emotion.

"What singular question!" said Mario. "I really believe that there is but one woman in the world who would address a man in such a way as that."

"It is not precisely about that that I wish to ask you," replied Regina, somewhat impatiently. "I wish only to know, my cousin, whether you are sufficiently frank to reply straightforwardly to the question I am about to ask you?"

"Why should I not?" said Mario.

"Ah!" replied Regina. "There may be reasons! Who can tell? There are some secrets that one conceals, and some that one confides only to certain persons. I am quite certain, Mario, that your sadness at this moment is caused by some secret which you conceal; and I cannot but ask myself why you hesitate to confide it to me—to me, who am more than your cousin, but your friend."

Mario remained some time without replying, then lifted his head, and, gazing steadily at Regina, calmly and without a trace of emotion, said:

"My dear cousin, it is possible that you have guessed rightly, and it is possible that you have fallen into an error. If I have kept some secret from you, it is because the secret is my own, and because I am unwilling that any of the persons who are dear to me should know it. But do not believe for a moment, Regina, that if I act thus, it is from any want of friendly feeling for you. As soon as I shall be able to tell my secret, if I have one,

I shall entrust it to you with all that feeling of confidence which I have ever had in you."

After Mario had spoken thus, he saluted Regina, and entered the fort.

There was nothing in these words which could give any certainty to Regina's suspicions; but she inferred from them that Mario was in love, and that she herself was not the object of that love.

Having reached this point, it was but a small step to infer further, that it was Alma whom he loved; and within the next fortnight, she had obtained all the proof necessary to confirm her conviction.

To say what then took place in her heart would be impossible.

Her breast was torn with tumultuous anguish, and she drank deeply of the cup of despair.

Alma became the object of her furious hate, and she lived only to take vengeance upon her.

To do this was not difficult.

She soon learned that Alma, who had been brought to the fortress while still an infant, was the daughter of Andrea's most hated enemy, and from that moment she had but one aim—but one desire—to inflict those evils upon Alma's father which she did not as yet venture to hurl against his daughter.

A mode of life, moreover, which should be full of unexpected incidents and mystery, perfectly suited her adventurous disposition. She eagerly seized upon the pretext of her enmity towards Alma's father, and became in a short time that Bel Demonio who had filled the province of Spoleto with terror far and wide.

IV. The Bad Angel

The sun had already been risen for an hour, when Regina traversed Andrea's camp and reentered the fortress.

"Our young lady is very early," said the people of the camp. "She must have risen this morning before the sun."

Regina dismounted from her horse in the courtyard. She wore her usual costume, a grey felt hat, and a black velvet jacket with silver buttons. Her calm, pale face betrayed no signs of fatigue.

She tossed Fuoco's bridle to a groom, and walked towards her apartments.

"It is strange," thought the groom to himself, as he rubbed down the black horse, which was covered with sweat and foam, "that whenever our young lady takes a morning ride, Fuoco returns in a state which would make one believe he had been twenty leagues without stopping. It Fuoco didn't have his stable to himself, I should be curious to see at what hour she sets out. What a proud woman she is! She never asks anyone to saddle her horse, and hold the bridle when she mounts."

While the honest groom thus reflected, Regina had arrived at her apartments; but before entering them, she came to face with Mario.

During the last few days, Mario had much changed; he was no longer the robust, joyous, carefree young man who had been wont to wander indolently around the mountains, with his hat to one side, and his musket on his shoulder, whistling a cheerful tune. He was no longer Mario the hunter, who preferred to hunt deer or red partridges for his cousins, than to mount guard at the advanced posts, and who would rather fight ten men than turn even slightly from his route.

Mario was now pale, somber, and reserved. He walked with hanging head, his hat low over his eyes, and performed his military duties with the most unusual care.

He set out from the fort in the morning, and never returned until evening, carefully avoiding the society of his father and Regina.

What did he do all the day, while his friends at the fortress were full of uneasiness about him? Lucrezia had told Alma that Mario often sat in that solitary spot amidst the mountains where he had so often sat side by side with the young girl; and there, indeed, with frowning brow, vague glance, and melancholy attitude, he lived over and over the memories of all the cherished days he had passed in the presence of Alma, until the sun sank beneath the horizon and he rose to return to the fort.

Mario had certainly changed greatly during the last few days. Seeing him thus, pale and sad, Regina stopped for a moment and bit her lip with anger.

A bitter smile passed over her countenance as she saluted him in a high and affected voice.

"Good day, cousin Mario!" she said, bowing with an air of exaggerated respect.

Mario, seeming neither to hear nor see her, walked on; but Regina seized him by the arm, and, pressing it with a vigorous and feverish grasp, repeated, in a bitter, imperative tone:

"Cousin Mario, good day!"

"Ah! Pardon, cousin!" said Mario, suddenly turning around, and taking no pains to conceal his annoyance. "Pardon! I did not see you."

"I suppose, cousin Mario, that you could not see me, because there is between you and me another face that you see too clearly."

"What do you mean?" asked Mario, with a troubled expression.

"And is it so, then?" replied Regina. "Has the daughter of our friend carried off with her not only the heart and reason of cousin Mario, but his sincerity also?"

"Good God, cousin!" exclaimed Mario, impatiently. "What are my heart, my reason, my sincerity to you? It is very strange, Regina, that you should devote so much of your attention to me, when this very night you have received such devoted homage from all the leading gentlemen of Spoleto! Have you not just returned from one of your habitual excursions?"

"Just so," replied Regina.

"Well, it was not cousin Mario that you went to seek there, I suppose?"

"No, Mario, you are right; but there was a time, which I remember well, though you may have forgotten it, when you would have been happy—you must acknowledge it yourself—to have been my cavalier, and to protect me against the attacks which might be directed against me. Then, Mario, you listened to all that I had to confide to you; and I, who trusted in you implicitly, concealed from you none of the secrets of my heart. That time seems very, very far away now."

These words were uttered in a tone which moved Mario. He gazed at Regina, and, struck by the unusual animation of her countenance, made a gentle gesture with his hand, and drew near to her.

"You are unjust, Regina," he said, earnestly and with a tone of genuine pity. "I love you, and shall always love you, as a brother. Your secrets shall never be betrayed by me, believe me; but as for protecting you, that would be, at present, thank God, a very superfluous effort on my part; for you have no need of protection. You are as strong as a man, Regina—as a man with a soul of well-tempered steel, and are more formidable than the most intrepid bandit of my father's troop."

Regina repressed an energetic gesture of anger, and kept sufficient self-control to be able to smile at Mario and thank him.

Without suspecting it for a moment, the latter had deeply wounded his cousin's heart; for Regina would have preferred, at that moment, Mario's utmost disdain to the fraternal affection which he offered her; and she felt it as a cruel wrong that he should remind her of that manly independence she was so fond of displaying, just at the moment when she so ardently desired to be in her cousin's eyes a woman.

She was resolved, however, not to appear humiliated; and so, presenting a bold front under this deadly blow, and casting a sparkling and angry glance at Mario, she replied:

"Well, my cousin, you wish to make common cause with our enemies? But if it is war that you want, you will not be surprised that I should endeavor to make my uncle, Andrea Vitelli, one of my auxiliaries?"

As she said this, Regina made an ironical salute to her cousin and went on her way, leaving Mario unable to conclude what he was to fear from this threat.

In the meantime, Regina proceeded towards her uncle's apartments, and was soon in his presence.

Andrea was still in bed, in that state which is between dreaming and waking. The imperious necessities of his duties kept him on foot during a portion of the night, and it was seldom that he could seek repose before the morning.

Regina approached his bed with light steps, and when she had reached Andrea's pillow, kissed gently on the forehead.

It needed only a slight touch to arouse Andrea, who started up in the manner of a man who fears a sudden attack.

When he perceived Regina beside him, the expression of distrust which had flashed over his countenance disappeared, and he attempted to smile as he said, in a tone of gentle reproach:

"Already up, my child? You are very early! Has something happened?"

"Nothing has happened," replied Regina, "except that I cannot sleep, and that it is long since I have been able to sleep."

"You suffer, then, my child?" exclaimed Andrea, in a tone of paternal solicitude.

"Yes, father."

"And what makes you suffer? Speak!"

"I dare not!"

"Can you not have confidence in me, my child, when I would give everything that I have in the world to ensure your happiness?"

"It is not you that I doubt, uncle, but Mario."

"Do not speak to me of Mario," interrupted Andrea. "Mario is no longer my child."

"Oh, pardon him a moment's passion! It is Alma, the daughter of our common enemy, who has caused all the evil."

"Yes," said the brigands' leader, as a frown gathered over his brow. "I have, in truth, committed a great mistake."

"Alas!" sighed Regina, "Mario loves Alma."

"What does it matter? There is an impassable gulf between them."

"But I, uncle…"

"Well?"

"I… I… love Mario."

A glance of joy passed over Andrea Vitelli's features as he heard these words, and he gazed delightedly at the young girl, who had hid her face in her hands.

"You love him?" he cried. "Is it possible? Ah! Then the wish of my poor sister will be realized, and I shall be able to fulfill her most cherished hope! Poor Regina, you love him, and do not dare to let him know it! Oh, be at ease with respect to the future, child. I wish that both you and he should be happy, and swear that you shall marry him."

And as Regina, intoxicated with joy, listened to him in silence, he continued, taking her hands in his own:

"Poor child! Why weep thus? This love of yours will be my sweetest consolation, as it has ever been the most sacred hope of my growing years. You love Mario? Well, Mario shall be yours!"

Regina possessed, in the highest degree, the talent of dissimulation; and, while the most exquisite pleasure suffused her heart at her uncle's words, her countenance betrayed no emotion, her eyes alone sparkling with a fire which, for a moment, threw a strange gleam upon her features.

She shook her head with an air of sadness as she replied:

"You forget that Mario does not love me! The daughter of our enemy has exercised here a strange influence. During long years she has paralyzed your hatred; the progress of time makes us forget many oaths;

and, thanks to his daughter, the Count is still, to this very day, a powerful man."

"It is so," murmured Andrea, pensively.

"And had it not been for this Bel Demonio, who seems sent by divine justice to take upon himself the task of your vengeance, Ercole, the traitor, the despoiler, would still be in the enjoyment of all his possessions. What is it that stays your arm, my uncle? Is it the affection that you feel for that girl, his daughter, or is it that you are afraid of her father?"

These words, pronounced by any other than Regina, would have raised a terrible tempest in Andrea's heart; but Regina was his well-beloved child. He turned pale, and said nothing.

Regina leaned forward towards him, so that her balmy breath passed like a warm spring breeze across his forehead, as she continued in a low, but animated voice:

"Uncle Andrea, if I were in your place—if I were as you are—a man, a warrior, brave and fearless—if I were that, uncle Andrea, things should not be as they are now!"

"Indeed!" replied the brigands' leader, smiling, as if he had wished to throw off the magnetic influence which had seized upon him.

That soft and virginal breath, that supple form which leaned against his breast, that feminine voice which murmured in his ear—all this exercised a fascination over Andrea's spirit—a sort of fascination against which it was impossible to struggle.

Regina noticed this, and resolved to consummate her victory. She bent her head forward, with a motion full of grace, in such a manner that her soft and glossy locks caressed her uncle's forehead.

Andrea threw his arm around her waist, and gazed upon the deep black eyes which magnetized his soul.

"Ah! If only I had a cuirass and a sword, as you have," said the young girl with an impetuous tone which thrilled his heart. "If I had a warrior's bold and indefatigable ardor, I would make this Ercole, before he died, curse the day when his mother conceived him! Is it for the sake of a little girl, uncle, that you have so soon forgotten all the outrages you have suffered? No! It shall never be said that your vow of vengeance was not fulfilled; and if you renounce it, my uncle—you, Andrea Vitelli—I myself will take it up and wage war upon Count Ercole, until not one stone of his last palace rests upon another!"

Andrea gave her a glance of pleasure mingled with admiration. His hand lost itself amidst the locks of her long hair, and from time to time, he involuntarily murmured:

"Beautiful demon!"

"Forward! Forward!" exclaimed Regina, in the clear girlish voice with which she had made the night ring on the mountain.

"It would give you pleasure?" asked Andrea, at length, half rising on his couch.

"Yes, uncle."

"You are jealous, my poor child!"

"Jealous of your honor, uncle!"

At these words a gleam of fire shot from the bandit's eyes. At once, he summoned Cosimo.

"See that the arms are put in order!" he cried, in the voice of a stentor, to his astonished subordinate. "Let the men and horses be ready for action. Tomorrow we shall resume work!"

"At last! At last!" said Regina, with a fierce joy in her heart.

V. The Handkerchief

Alma was so terrified by the appearance of Bel Demonio on the ramparts that she resolved to have Marina sleep in her chamber from then on.

The young masked cavalier and his twelve followers in their white mantles were ever present in her imagination; and such is the power of the mind, that the timid child thought at every instant that she saw some specter before her The old castle of Ercole, with its lofty walls, its deep moats, and the night birds lodged in its turrets, filled her with a vague sense of terror, for which she could not account, but against which the formidable garrison of the castle was no defense.

On the following morning, Marina, delighted at the arrangement, placed her bed in a corner of her mistress's chamber. She was charmed at being Alma's company, as she was the only girl of her own age in the fort. Despite their difference in rank, she felt herself attracted to Alma by that need of affection which is so natural to young girls.

When the night's ablutions were finished, the mistress and maid went to their beds; but it is scarcely necessary to say, rather to talk than to sleep. Marina, especially, was an indefatigable chatterbox. She knew everything about the castle and its environs; she knew all the stories of the plain and the mountains; and it was a genuine pleasure to her to be allowed to bestow upon her young mistress some of the stores of her memory.

Cradled by her maid's gentle voice, Alma had begun to feel sleep pressing on her weary lids, when suddenly the sound of a hunting horn aroused her.

"Do you hear that?" she asked Marina, as she half raised herself from her pillow.

"Yes, Mademoiselle," replied Marina, "and I must say that to hear a hunting horn at this time of night astonishes me. There was once in this part of the region an old hunter, a great signor, named Roland de Montecavallo, who was a very demon of a hunter; but old Roland is dead, and besides, it is night, and it is not the custom for hunters to pursue…"

"Hush! Hush!" interrupted Alma. "You prevent my hearing!"

Marina, forced to be silent, listened with her mistress.

The horn sounded a *fanfare* more monotonous than brilliant, and the plaintive notes of the instrument expired on the silence of the night, like the voice of a lover under his mistress's window.

"It is not lively," said Marina.

"Hush! Hush!" repeated Alma.

The two young girls remained silent, and could now easily perceive that the notes of the horn were coming closer.

"Shall we look out?" asked Alma, with an air of attention and curiosity.

"Look out?" cried Marina. "Pray don't think of such a thing, Mademoiselle! Suppose we were to see that frightful Bel Demonio?"

Alma was moved and pensive. The sound of the horn at this hour of the night filled her soul with gentle reveries; for it was not the first time that she had heard the mountain tune which the blower of the born was playing, and it reminded her of many sweet moments. She blushed in the shade, sighed, and timidly raised herself.

"My faith!" said Marina, following her example "I think I should like to see, too!"

"No, remain where you are," involuntarily exclaimed Alma. "If there is anything to see, I will tell you."

Marina was one who always wanted to do a thing as soon as she was forbidden to do it.

She obeyed her young mistress, however, although sorely against her will.

Alma drew aside the curtains and looked out.

The night was clear and limpid, as Italian nights almost always are. The moon and the stars sparkled in the azure like spangles of gold and silver on a velvet mantle. The warm breeze of the summer night sighed along the valley, awaking gentle murmurs amongst its groups of trees. The moon seemed to have descended to the bosom of the marshes, as, in the mythological times, Diana, its goddess, was wont to descend with her nymphs to bathe in the clearest fountains, before she went alone, by secret paths, to the depths of the woods, to meet the shepherd Endymion.

It was one of those splendid nights written about by Salvator [16] in his admirable *canzones*, during which the

---

[16] Salvator Rosa (1615-1673) was an Italian Baroque painter, poet, musician, and printmaker, active in Naples, Rome, and Florence. During the commencement of his studies under his brother-in-law Francanzani in Naples, Della Valle, one of his contemporaries, spoke of the female musicians Signorine Leonora and Caterina, "who were never heard but with rapture, particularly the elder, who accompanied herself on the arch lute. I remember their mother in her youth, when she sailed in her felucca near the grotto of Pausilippo, with her golden harp in her hand; but in our times these shores were inhabited by

Caterina and the White Leonora, cradled in their feluccas on the gulf of Naples, awoke with songs the sonorous echoes of Pausilippo,[17] or held amorous discourse with the pagan cardinals of Urban VIII.

Even the sentinel had submitted to the dreamy influence of this glorious night, and, having thrown down his musket, was stretched and asleep upon the bastion's turf, dreaming doubtless of some brown peasant girl from Friuli.

At first the valley appeared to Alma to be utterly deserted; and although she listened as attentively as possible, she could no longer hear the melancholy notes of the hunting horn. However, she did not allow herself to be discouraged by this first disappointment; and, after some minutes' continued attention, she saw a man climbing up the bastion on which the sentinel lay asleep, towards the part of the castle in which she was.

This man looked about him with an uneasy air, and then perceiving, doubtless, that there was no obstacle in his way, took some steps in advance, crossed his arms, and began to attentively inspect the approach to Count Ercole's old castle.

The light of the moon fell full upon the face of the stranger, who was but a very short distance from Alma's window; and as the young girl, inspired, doubtless, by some divine instinct, leaned forward eagerly to examine his features, she suddenly grew pale, and drew back with a cry.

"Good Heavens!" exclaimed Marina, jumping out of bed. "What is the matter, Mademoiselle?"

---

syrens, not only beautiful and tuneful, but virtuous and beneficent."
[17] Residential quarter of Naples.

"Nothing, nothing!" said Alma, confused and embarrassed. "Go to bed again, child. It is nothing."

"Oh, but I want to see what has so frightened Mademoiselle!"

"It is nothing, I tell you—nothing! Go to bed again, Marina! I want to open the window—the night is fine, and I want some air."

Alma was forced to take Marina by the hand and lead her back to her couch, and the young girl, yielding, went to her bed, but resolved to leave it again at the first opportunity.

Then Alma immediately returned to the window and opened it. The noise she made in doing this attracted the stranger's attention for he no sooner perceived Alma at the casement than he, in his turn, uttered a cry of joy.

He immediately measured with his eye the depth of the fortress' moat, and began to descend it. The slope was steep, the grass short, and the earth damp. As he descended, he aided himself with his dagger; but when he had reached the end of the slope, he found a wall twenty feet-high, in such a state of decay that it threatened to tumble down.

In climbing this, the stranger ran an imminent risk of breaking his legs; but nothing stopped him, and at length he reached the level ground in safety.

Alma followed him with her eyes with increasing anxiety, every now and then glancing at the sentinel, who continued to sleep, dreaming of a crowd of peasant girls both fair and dark.

The stranger advanced rapidly, and, without hesitation, entered the wet portion of the moat. The water reached up to his waist, and his feet sank deep in the mud; but he triumphed over this obstacle, as he had triumphed over the others, and when he had reached the opposite bank, he ran joyfully beneath the window at which stood the young girl.

"Alma!" he cried.

"Mario!" she responded, with an emotion she could not repress.

"Ah!" cried Marina, jumping out of bed. "I heard someone speaking, I am sure."

She turned her eyes towards the moat before Alma could stop her.

"A man!" she cried.

"Oh, hush, hush!" said Alma, clasping her hands together. "Hush! I entreat you. It is my cousin Mario. Oh, hush! For should the sentinel awake, he would kill him!"

"Never fear, Mademoiselle!" cried Marina, whose eyes sparkled like two stars, and whose face took on a comic expression of gravity. "Since it is your cousin Mario, and since you love him…"

"But I did not say that," said Alma, reddening and trembling. "Yes, he is my cousin, and I love him—that is to say, I do not love him…"

"I am not the one to give pain to two persons who love each other," interrupted Marina, looking forward with pleasure to the chance of playing the part of confidant. "And if Mademoiselle will permit me, I will stand by the door, lest that Old Mercedes should come spying."

"No, Marina, no!" said Alma. "The door is closed; we have nothing to fear on that side; and, besides, my cousin is just going; so go back to bed, my child, and let me persuade him to go."

Marina pensively regained her bed; but deep in her heart, she was happy—she did not know why.

A lover! That word makes young girls dream.

While Marina was regaining her couch, Alma had gone back to the window.

"Alma, Alma!" cried Mario, when he saw her reappear. "How happy it makes me to see you! Ah! Since your departure, I have been so sad! Oh, if you only knew how sad…"

"I also am very happy," said the girl, blushing. "Very happy to see you again, now that we are separated forever. But believe me, my dear friend, you have committed a great imprudence in coming here. It is not for my own sake that I speak, Mario, for it matters very little what anyone thinks of me, but for you, Mario. The sentinel might awake, and I could not save you."

"How good you are to think of me!" said Mario.

"Alas!" replied Alma, "the thought of you is ever in my heart. That is more than I ought to say; but why should my heart lie? No, Mario, I will tell you without fear and without shame, that since I left the mountain I have not stopped thinking of you; but it is necessary to be prudent, and not to provoke new misfortunes."

But Mario, lifting up his two hands towards Alma in supplication, without giving the least thought to the sentinel, or the dangers of which the young girl spoke, said:

"When you were in the mountains, Alma, I did not know how much I loved you; but ever since your departure, I have understood what has taken place in my heart, and today, I know that I love you and that I cannot live without you."

"Why do you speak thus, Mario? I have told you, and you know it, that an impassable gulf separates us now, and God only knows when this abyss will be filled! But pray, pray do not tempt fate anymore; I am filled with terror at the idea that some catastrophe may happen. Mario, Mario, pray go!"

"Yes, you are right," replied Mario. "Everything is against us, and an abyss does indeed separate us. You are right! We can never belong to each other; and yet, Alma, how is it that, in spite of this conviction, in spite of the fates that are against us, how is it that at this very moment I feel full of energy and hope? Oh, no, no! Alma, is it not possible that even if God should wish to separate us, a power greater than that of men will save us, and our love will still inspire us with resources, by means of which we may obtain the fulfillment of our hopes."

Alma sadly shook her head, and threw an uneasy glance towards the bastion.

The sentinel still slept.

The poor child would have wished to have asked after Regina and Andrea, but she was afraid of prolonging their meeting.

In the meantime, Marina, with open eyes and ears, had made incredible efforts to hear what was being said.

"Ah! Well," said Alma, after a moment's silence, "may God hear and grant our prayers, Mario! And I will confess to you that if God should ever bless our union, it will be the happiest day of my life. But go, my friend, do not wait a moment longer in this dangerous place. And when you return to the mountain, tell your father that I shall never forget him, and assure Regina that I shall always love her."

"Oh! Do not speak of Regina," said Mario. "She is a monster rather than a woman! Until now I have kept her secret, but one day you shall know all."

"What do you mean?" asked Alma, to whom these words were an impenetrable mystery.

"Do not ask me questions today," replied Mario. "Only let me tell you that I love you..."

"Mario," interrupted Alma, "you are right. I will not question you now, for I know that any moment might cause some terrible catastrophe. If you love me, Mario, dear Mario, go! I beg you."

"Well," at length said the young man, "I will go, but before I do, Alma, dearest Alma, let me carry away some souvenir which I may constantly retain as a gage of our love."

Alma hesitated a moment, and then, leaning gently from the window, and looking around to see that there was no one watching, she let fall her handkerchief.

"I have nothing but that," she said with a smile overflowing with happiness. "It dried many tears; and, in reminding you of my grief, it will remind you of my love."

"Oh! Thank you, thank you!" cried Mario, kissing it a thousand times. "With this talisman upon my heart, I shall fear nothing in all the world."

"And now, pray go!" said Alma.

"I will go now; but in three days I shall return at the same hour."

"Pray do not."

"In three days," repeated Mario, as he departed hastily, so as not to leave Alma time to forbid him.

Alma's eyes followed him with the deepest anxiety.

He passed the marsh, not without difficulty; and when he had reached the other side, he turned and murmured that sweet, but melancholy Italian word: "*Addio!*"

Then he climbed the wall, scrambled up the slope, and gained the bastion.

When there, he made another sign of farewell to the young girl, who still followed him with her anxious glance, and then plunged with hasty steps into the valley.

Alma felt her heart relieved of an enormous weight.

Sighing, she closed the window and sat down, sad and pensive, by the side of her bed.

"He has gone, then?" asked Marina.

"Yes," replied Alma.

"And when will he return?"

"In three days, perhaps; but be discreet, my child, for if what passed this evening were to be known, the greatest evils would result."

"Oh! Mademoiselle, be at ease," replied Marina. "I would have my tongue cutout before I would say a word. Me, say a word about a matter of love? I would rather…"

"Sleep, sleep!" interrupted Alma, going once more to bed.

Marina slept little that night and Alma not much more. She thought of Mario; she thought of the strange words he had spoken with respect to Regina, and wondered what the mystery to which he had alluded.

"Regina… A monster?" she murmured.

At last, she slept, and dreamed during the rest of the night of the masked cavalier, followed by the horsemen in the white mantles.

In her dream it seemed to her that the cavalier's mask fell off, and revealed the face of Regina. She uttered a cry, and awoke.

"Ah!" said Marina, who had not the least inclination to sleep. "I'll wager that Mademoiselle is dreaming of her cousin!"

VI. The Wound

On the following day, Count Ercole's castle wore an unusual air of festivity.

In the morning, a courier arrived from Spoleto with a letter from the Marquis of Santa Fiore, which he had no doubt would spread joy throughout the mansion.

In this missive, the Marquis of Santa Fiore demanded of Prince Ercole Vitelli the hand of his daughter in marriage.

The Marquis spoke of immediate nuptials, earnestly desiring, he said, to have the marriage concluded as soon as possible.

There was a postscript, in which the Marquis gave the Prince the most earnest advice with respect to his pack, so that it might be kept in a good state, and rendered fit to again hunt for wild boars within a very short time.

This letter, as may be supposed, filled Prince Ercole with pleasure, since it promised him the realization of one of his dearest hopes. It promised him both the restoration of the fortunes of his house, and powerful protection against the attacks of his enemy.

As soon Alma had descended from her room, he asked her to meet him in his office.

"My child," said Ercole, with a smile upon his lips, "I have some good news to tell you."

"What it, father?" asked Alma, astonished.

"As soon as you were restored to me, I began to consider how I might secure your happiness."

"My happiness?"

"Your future, at least. I have planned a marriage."

"A marriage for me?" exclaimed Alma, growing pale.

Then, making an effort to overcome her timidity, she added, gently shaking her head:

"I think, father, that you have been quite mistaken as to what could render me happy; for the idea of marriage has never entered my head."

The Old Prince knit his brows, be dryly replied:

"You reject my proposal, then, without even knowing whom I have chosen for your husband. May I know, at least, what is the reason that you makes you act thus?"

"I have no reason," murmured Alma, blushing.

"Then I cannot understand you," continued the old man, in cool, dry tone. "The Marquis of Santa Fiore has demanded of me your hand in marriage, and I have this morning accepted his offer."

"Father! Father!" cried Alma, falling at his knees "Spare me! I do not know the Marquis of Santa Fiore; I have only seen him once; I cannot love him. Spare me, father! Spare me!"

Count Ercole had not expected this resistance, and it made him deeply angry. For a moment, he was on the point of playing his assumed character of father in earnest; for he felt himself moved by the great tears which were flowing down Alma's cheeks. But that good sentiment lasted all too briefly. He said to himself:

"Bah! After all, she is only Lucrezia Mammone's daughter."

Then, turning towards Alma, he said, in a manner which brooked of no reply:

"Child, you have been in this house but a very few days, and you are ignorant of our habits; but you will, probably, have already remarked, that when Count Ercole commands, the heads and wills of those about

193

him are bent in submission to his word. I repeat, then, Alma, that the Marquis of Santa Fiore has asked for your hand, that I have consented to his request, and that I desire you to be ready to become his wife."

Alma had no strength to reply, and retired to her chamber bathed in tears.

"My God! My God!" cried Marina, seeing her mistress in this state. "What has happened, Mademoiselle?"

"Go, my child! Leave me alone!"

"But he will come again in three days," persisted the young girl, who knew nothing of what had just taken place.

"Alas! Alas!" thought poor Alma "When he returns, what shall I have to tell him?"

And she fell into a chair, overwhelmed with emotions, her head in her hands, and her heart full of misery and tears.

In the meantime, old Count Ercole was more joyous than he had been for a long time; and he ordered that the soldiers should be served with a double ration of wine.

That evening, the whole fort resembled a huge tavern, and from the cellars to the garrets, there was nothing but singing and boisterous mirth.

A sumptuous table had been laid out in the handsomest apartment in the castle, on which the most generous wines from the cellars sparkled in the most exquisitely chased cups.

Count Ercole did the honors at his table with an air of enjoyment which he had never before displayed, and seemed to have grown young again.

The prospect of this powerful alliance had, for a moment, banished from his heart the fears with which it was generally oppressed.

The officers of the garrison drank deeply, and laughed loudly.

There were moments, indeed, when the walls echoed with so much noise, that the arched roof vibrated and seemed on the point of collapsing.

Capitan, Pasquale Contarini, and his graciousness Tiberio Fanferluizzi had never been more exuberant or more attired.

Capitan had had his moustache in curl-papers all morning, and had polished up his armor in such a manner that the best warrior of that poet of chivalry, Ariosto,[18] would have appeared but a mean soldier of fortune beside him.

Tiberio had drunk—drunk much; perhaps even a little too much. He recited verses in the style of Petrarch, and shed tears into his glass. Bows and rosettes pleasantly adorned his velvet doublet, and altogether he presented a picture of elegance and sentimentality, bathed in wine, which reminded one of a German dream, and would have formed a very appropriate subject for Hoffman.[19]

Signor Pasquale never said a word for fear of spilling, like an overfull goblet; however, his nose spoke the most eloquent language of drunkenness it is possible to imagine, and darted forth fiery gleams which could only

---

[18] Ludovico Ariosto (1474-1533), an Italian poet best known for his chivalrous epic *Orlando Furioso* (1516). The poem describes the adventures of Charlemagne, Orlando, and the Franks as they battle against the Saracens.

[19] Ernst Theodor Amadeus Hoffman (1776-1822), a Prussian Romantic author of fantasy and Gothic horror tales, as well as a composer. His stories highly influenced 19th-century literature, and he is one of the major authors of the Romantic Movement.

be compared to those with which a ruby sparkles when touched by a ray of light.

"Yes, gentlemen," said the Old Prince, "my castle is about to become once more a joyful house; and we shall resume, please God, our legitimate authority over the province. We shall soon see whether we continue to be affronted as we have hitherto been, when the house of Santa Fiore is allied with the princely house of Vitelli!"

"Gentlemen," cried the sentimental Tiberio Fanferluizzi, "I propose a toast to the moon! Yes, to the moon, the goddess of love!"

As he uttered these words, the honorable Signor Tiberio Fanferluizzi tottered upon his legs, and, having poured the contents of his glass upon his frill, fell back upon his chair, and burst into tears.

"By my ancestors!" cried Contarini. "This is a pleasant joke!"

"The Devil!" said Capitan. "I would rather drink to the health of Achilles, or Leonidas, the hero of the Thermopylæ!"

Contarini drank a great glass at a draught, in sign of satisfaction.

Capitan twisted his moustache, and struck the table with his fist.

"To the noble Marquis of Santa Fiore!" cried the old Prince at the same time rising on his legs.

All the guests imitated their host, and repeated his words.

The glasses were filled and emptied.

It was now near midnight; the lamps had begun to burn less vividly, and to give out a somber red light. The vast hall in which the festival was held seemed still vaster than it really was, for the shadows which began to gather in its corners covered its outlines, and gave it an air of mystery.

In the midst of this vast chamber, now filled with shifting shadows, was a white table, covered with wine-stains, and the scattered remains of a feast, around which hovered the strange-looking forms of the drinkers.

Some of them, pale and haggard as specters, endeavored in vain to recover their drunken senses; whilst others, rubicund and joyful, poured forth in profusion the sparkling follies of intoxication.

The wearied servants slept in corners, and on the benches of the antechamber.

The guests who were still able to speak exchanged a thousand confidences—joyous or sad, serious or happy, according to the degree in which they were drunk.

Tiberio confessed that he had never written a single one of all the sonnets which he was so fond of reciting as his own.

Pasquale Contarini spoke of his noble ancestors, and cited, amongst others, his father the tailor, and his grandfather the cobbler.

Signor Capitan recounted to his neighbor how he had been put in a terrible fright one evening, when he was alone, by his housekeeper knocking at his door, and asking him whether he had not heard somebody cry, "Thieves, thieves!"

Others made confessions of cruel revenge, unfair combat, perfidies, crimes... Oh, humanity!

Count Ercole alone kept his secrets; for he had secrets so terrible that the most indiscreet drunkenness could not drag them from his heart.

But, in fact, Ercole was not drunk. Men who have committed monstrous actions, crime of more than ordinary enormity, keep control over themselves.

And, even if he had wished to make himself drunk, as a means of forgetting himself, drunkenness itself, that terrible draught of forgetfulness, which Manfred so earnestly implored, fled from his cup,[20] and would not cross the threshold of his lips.

Ercole, we said, was not drunk, but the warm Italian wine had warmed his old blood. He had the prospect now of some measure of security in the future, of enjoying an oasis in that journey of life which had hitherto been for him such a dreary desert. He found himself, as if by a miracle, suddenly young, strong, and happy.

He rose and said:

"Gentlemen, I am a henceforth a free and happy man!"

"Soul and body!" shouted Capitan. "I should like to see anyone attack your liberty!"

"Diana of the silver horns…" began Fanferluizzi.

"The gurgling of the bottles is a thousand times more musical than the murmur of brooks," yelped Contarini.

"Be quiet there, pagans!" said Capitan, "and allow his lordship to speak!"

On this there was a moment's silence, which was only broken by the snoring of the greater part of the guests.

"We shall now see," 'said the old Prince, "whether I shall any longer be the sport of my enemies."

"Yes, yes, we shall see!" said Capitan.

"Now, now!" continued the old man, "now let Andrea come to this castle, filled with brave soldiers, and surrounded by strong walls!"

---

[20] Alluding to Lord Byron's eponymous 1817 poem.

"Ah, ah, my Prince! Bravely spoken!" shouted Capitan. "A good jest, forsooth, to suppose that that Andrea would venture to show himself here, whilst I, Capitan, vanquisher of the Turks, am here!"

"Andrea, Andrea!" shouted Ercole, in a paroxysm of exultation, and with an expression of savage hate, "I detest you and I despise you!"

Count Ercole had scarcely uttered these words when the door of the banqueting hall was flung open with great clamor, and Andrea Vitelli, sword in hand, with pale face and sparkling eye, appeared upon the threshold.

"Ercole!" he said, in a deep, sonorous voice, "you have defied me; here I am!"

Capitan immediately sank under the table.

The other guests gazed on their host with a terrified, stupefied stare.

Ercole himself seemed rooted the spot in which he stood. Stupefaction and terror prevented him from flying. His tongue, glued to his palate, could utter no sound.

With three steps Andrea reached his side.

"Ercole!" he said, in his loud, firm voice. "There is a terrible account to settle between us! We shall meet again! Your friends are as cowardly as yourself! You summoned me, and all those who ought to have been ready to defend you are either drunk or terrified. Ercole! Never again defy Andrea Vitelli!"

As he spoke thus, Andrea raised his sword with a terrible gesture, and cut the sign of a cross upon the old man's face.

Ercole uttered a hideous yell. All the guests half rose from their seats, with open mouths and drawn swords.

Ercole sank down upon his feeble limbs, shaking his disfigured and bleeding face, and shouting:

"Help! Help! Guards, help!"

"I am here!" said Capitan, rising from beneath the table.

He had seen Andrea depart, and this circumstance had not a little contributed to reanimate his courage.

He ran to the soldiers' quarters, and cried:

"To arms!"

But unfortunately, the soldiers, wrapped in sleep, awoke but slowly.

A guard, however, made the round of the castle, and carefully inspected the moats.

When it reached the drawbridge, it was found lowered.

The men in charge had taken flight.

VII. The Ambush

Count Ercole's wound was not serious, but was certain to disfigure him as long as he lived. The most skillful surgeon could not remove that fateful cross, which only served to prove how powerless the Prince of Monteleone of the province of Spoleto was against an enemy out of reach of the law.

Ercole writhed upon his bed of pain, uttering cries of rage, cursing those around him, cursing himself, and invoking all the powers of Hell.

Mercedes alone watched over him. The maladies of the old Count were the most formidable trials which the minister of the Divine wrath had ever inflicted upon the old duenna.

Ercole had now become hard, cruel, and implacable towards his accomplice.

"You are the cause of all my misfortunes!" he constantly exclaimed. "It is you whom Heaven should punish!"

"Alas, alas, Signor!" she replied, kneeling beside his bed. "In what I did, I only obeyed you."

"It was you who held the pillow!"

"But you who poured out the poison."

"It you who made him drink it—you!"

"Because I was afraid you would have killed me if I had not done it."

"Oh, misery, misery!"

The old Prince writhed, full of anger and powerless wrath, while the duenna prayed to Heaven for mercy.

They were terrible scenes, the whole horror of which the pen is inadequate to describe. At certain times the old Count and his accomplice dared not look each other in the face. It more than remorse that they suffered. It was as if they endured in this world a foretaste of the flames of Hell.

In the meantime the soldiers kept strict watch without. The sentinels had been doubled. The care of the drawbridge had been entrusted to one of the officers of the fort. At his order alone could the portcullis to be lowered or raised.

These military precautions greatly alarmed Alma, who watched with terror the approach of the day which Mario had fixed for his second visit.

On the third day, she retired to her chamber at an early hour. Marina followed her. The lady's maid was not as cheerful as usual. She said but little, and a slight frown was visible on her young, fifteen year-old forehead.

Marina had her own reasons for being anxious, but they were doubtless of a private nature, for she did not think it proper to communicate them to her young mistress. She sat on the edge of her bed, her chin in her hand, her head bending forwards.

Daylight had begun to fade, and the descending shadows of night half hid the valley of Marcia from view, like those transparent gauzes with which the young girls of Italy veil their pure and radiant countenances.

The nightingales had begun to sing; the gnats still performed their fantastic waltzes and quadrilles in the air. A distant bell sounded harmoniously at the bottom of the valley.

Alma knelt down and prayed.

"Holy Virgin," she said, "and Thou, Divine Jesus, send some good angel down into the valley to guide the steps of Mario home, away from this mansion full of soldiers!"

Alma had not lit her lamp. Sitting by the open window, she had followed, with an uneasy, anxious glance, the fading of the daylight, and the falling shadows or night.

The moon arose, white and tremulous on the horizon, like a nymph who issues naked and shivering from a crystal fountain. The moon, which inspires poets with dreams, makes dogs bark and infants stare, and is the confidant of lovers, appeared mysterious between two dark firs on a mountain slope.

For the first time in her life, Alma hated the heavenly body, and longed for a starless night.

"O Night," she said to herself, "for this once, leave in your jewel case your diamond planets, your opal stars, and all the precious jewels of gold and silver with which you delight to adorn your brow. Mario is coming, and Mario has need of darkness and mystery."

But the night was inexorable.

Nine o'clock sounded on the castle clock, and immediately afterwards, there was a movement along the ramparts. The captains of the guard were relieving the sentinels.

There was nothing extraordinary in this, as Alma well knew; but still it filled her with a strong sentiment of fear. Why is it that the heart trembles so at certain hours of the night? From where come those presentments which sometimes besiege the mind? Can young girls ever answer such questions? They dream or sing, weep or laugh, like the birds of the woods. Sometimes, because the sunlight falls in showers of gold through the fragrant thickets; sometimes, because the breeze sighs harmoniously through the crests of the trees. And just now, Alma was in that state in which fear changes every-thing to our mind.

Before quitting his post, the sentinel exchanged a few words in a low voice with his successor.

To Alma, this seemed an important circumstance. It appeared to her also that the sentinels generally spoke together longer than was necessary for the exchange of the countersign.

All this, although there was nothing in it, disquieted her extremely; and she turned impatiently towards Marina, who, contrary to her custom, was not babbling.

"How is it, then, Marina," she said, "that you are not talking this evening?"

"I am listening, Mademoiselle," replied the little maid. "It seems to me as if I could definitely hear the hunting horn in the distance."

"It not yet time," replied Alma, trembling.

"It is nine o'clock" observed Marina. "I do not know how it is that the day has appeared so frightfully long to me."

"I am terrified," said Alma. "Since the dreadful af-fair of the other night, everyone in the castle seems to be on guard."

"All the soldiers have loaded their muskets."

"I pray that Mario will not come."

"As do I," said Marina, sighing.

The two girls fell silent. They listened for a moment with the most profound attention. The valley was com-pletely still. No sound, no signal reached their ears.

"Ah!" exclaimed Alma, "if the sentinel would but sleep, as he did before."

"Ah! I wish he would," replied Marina, "but I fear that they are watched more strictly these last three days."

To the great surprise of the two young girls, they had scarcely finished speaking when the sentinel at the foot of the ramparts placed his musket against a tree and stretched himself on the grass, as his comrade had done three days before, to dream of the peasant girls of Friuli,

In a few moments the soldier appeared to be soundly asleep.

"God has had pity on us," exclaimed Alma, clasping her hands together, with a naive and gentle fervor.

"We are saved!" cried Marina.

And then, as if she had but awaited this incident, she suddenly became as she had been three days before—that is to say, inquisitive and chattering.

Alma herself, preoccupied as she was, could not help but remark on this change.

"You are very strange," she said with a slight smile. "A few moments ago you did not say a word, and now you are a total chatterbox."

"Since the soldier has gone to sleep," said Marina, slightly embarrassed, "it seems to me as though a great weight has been lifted from my heart."

"Then you were as frightened as I was?"

"Yes. The preparations made by the soldiers frightened me. But now, I am no longer afraid."

"Ah!" said Alma, shaking pretty bend, "but I would still give much not to have Mario come tonight!"

"Listen! Listen!" suddenly interrupted Marina, starting.

If Alma had looked at her just then, she would have been startled by the sudden change which came over her face.

But Alma had neither time nor inclination to observe her; for at that moment, she heard the sound of a horn, which sent its sonorous echoes through the valley.

It was the mountain tune, full of melancholy and wild originality, of which Mario was so fond.

"It is he!" said Alma.

The two young girls listened, and the notes of the horn continued.

"Oh, my God, protect him!" murmured Alma. As she sunk down on her knees to pray.

Marina, kneeling beside her small couch, prayed also.

It was a strange thing to see these two young girls praying at the hour appointed for a love meeting.

The prayer on each side was earnest, and Marina threw a fervor into hers at which Alma was astonished.

A loud and prolonged fanfare at length told them that Mario was close at hand.

Alma trembled. As if by a sympathetic beat, every note drew from her heart a sigh, and bitter tears flowed down her cheeks.

She was frightened. The sentinel was within a hundred and he might hear! Nevertheless, although the notes of the horn made the echoes resound, the sentinel did not wake. He paid not the slightest attention to it, and did not even raise his head from his pillow of turf.

"All goes well!" murmured Marina, who, even paler and more anxious than Alma, watched the sleeping sentinel with the utmost attention.

And, in fact, all did go well; for the last notes of the horn were still quivering in the air when Mario leaped upon the parapet.

His elegant person, illumined from behind by the moon, stood out against the dark background of the plain.

He waved his hat in the air, and advanced to the edge of the parapet. It a critical moment.

Alma leaned eagerly forward from the window, and motioned to him not to advance.

But Mario pointed to the sentinel with a smile, because the man still slept, and shook his head.

He continued to advance, without heeding Alma's suppliant gestures, and speedily reached the slope of the moat.

Marina said nothing, but kept close to her window, immoveable and pale in her fear as a statue.

Her eyes never left the sleeping sentinel.

"Imprudent!" murmured Alma, as she perceived Mario still advancing.

In fact, the latter had now reached the wall. He placed his dagger between two stones, seized hold of its handle with a vigorous grasp, and endeavored to catch hold with his feet of the broken edges of the wall.

This wall was, as we have already said, in a terrible condition, and was very likely to fall at the least false movement.

Mario was, therefore, quite imprudent to choose this way of advancing in the direction he wished, and the result proved it; for, the moment when he planted his foot in one of the hollows of the wall, some of the stones of which it was composed loosened, and fell to the ground with a great noise. Some of them rolled even as far as the moat, and fell into it with an immense splash.

"Oh, Heavens!" exclaimed Alma, clasping her two hands to her heart. "He is lost!"

"Holy Virgin!" cried Marina.

But, nevertheless, the sentinel never stirred, but remained buried in the deepest slumber.

Mario, suspended for a moment, preserved his presence of mind, and sought a fresh support for his feet. He tried it well before trusting his weight to it, and descended at last without fresh mishap.

"Ah!" said Alma, raising her hands to heaven, "it is plain that God is with him!"

Mario now crossed the moat as on the previous occasion, and walked in the water up to his waist.

He had soon passed through it, and stood beneath Alma's window.

"Cousin," he said, "I am here!"

But Alma had not time to reply before Marina uttered a fearful scream.

She had seen the sentinel suddenly rise, and not in the manner of man who awakes from sleep.

"Fly!" she cried, leaning forth towards Mario.

"Fly! Fly!" repeated Alma, without understanding the greatness of the danger.

Mario, who could not see the sentinel, hesitated.

"Fly!" repeated Marina, as pale as death.

Mario looked around him, and comprehended at length that some serious danger threatened him. No sign of fear, however, appeared on his countenance; for it was not the first time he had been in danger, and he knew how to face it.

He grasped his dagger and threw himself suddenly into the moat. But his very haste was against him, for the water plants clung to his legs, and he found himself suddenly stopped.

"My God!" cried Alma. "He doesn't move!"

Marina was, for her part, as anxious and disquieted as her mistress.

Standing beside the latter, and without uttering a single word, she followed with her eyes all the sentinel's movements.

She saw him stoop, pick up his musket, and discharge it in the air.

Poor Marina fell on her knees, while Alma uttered a cry, and hid her face in her hands.

Mario turned pale, for he realized that he was a lost man.

By a desperate effort, however, he gained the bank, only to find himself surrounded by soldiers, who had hastened to the spot at the signal.

Mario reflected for moment, and glanced at the muskets pointed against him.

At the second summons, he threw down his dagger with a gesture full of bitterness and disdain.

The soldiers, who had apparently only waited for this, immediately fell upon Mario and began to drag him away.

Before falling into their hands, however, he had had time to turn to Alma, who was gazing, trembling and dismayed, at what was taking place, and he said in a low voice:

"Do not be too sorry for me, Alma, for now we shall at least be near each other!"

Alma remained for some time plunged in a dumb, but terrible grief, neither speaking nor weeping; but when she saw Mario, dragged along by the soldiers, disappear from before her; when at length she came to herself, she passed her hand convulsively across her forehead, and perceived little Marina half insensible at her feet.

Alma had the kindest heart in the world, and had sufficient self-control to subdue her own grief for the purpose of soothing that which appeared to overwhelm her maid.

She endeavored to question Marina, but could only obtain from her disconnected, meaningless words.

When she went to bed, despair and anxiety kept her long awake, and when at last she slept, she was tormented by horrible dreams.

At last a nightmare awoke her.

She heard Marina tossing in her own bed. The child was endeavoring to stifle her sobs by biting her lips.

Alma feigned not to hear; but this protracted and excessive grief caused her to reflect.

It was certainly extraordinary that person to whom Mario was unknown should be so grieved on his account...

VIII. The Escape

Almost every day, when the sun had disappeared behind the Apennines, Alma went out of the fort, and walked for about an hour.

In general, Mercedes or Marina accompanied her; but, when she did not go beyond the outer line of the fortifications, she went alone.

Since Mario's imprisonment, Alma had not left her chamber; and had felt no inclination to do so.

The castle, however, seemed to her so melancholy, since she knew that Mario was imprisoned there, that, towards the end of the second day, she went out of the fortress alone.

It was God, doubtless, who had inspired her to do this; for she had advanced but a short distance, when a woman passed like a shadow between a thicket which bordered the road, and advanced straight towards her.

It was Lucrezia Mammone.

"Oh, how glad I am to meet you!" exclaimed Lucrezia when she perceived her. "For two days, I have been looking for you; wandering around the castle in the hopes of meeting you."

"Is something wrong?" quickly demanded Alma.

"Unless my heart deceives me," replied Lucrezia, "a great danger threatens you."

"Me?" said Alma, shaking her head. "You must mean Mario?"

"I know that Mario is a prisoner," replied Lucrezia, "but it is not to him that I allude. Regina…"

"Has any misfortune happened to her?"

"Oh, no," replied Lucrezia, "but Regina is not what you think her!"

"What do you mean?"

"Oh, my child! Regina, your cousin, whom you love so, and whom you have been accustomed to call your sister, is none other than that fantastic brigand who has terrified the whole province with his crimes."

"Bel Demonio?" murmured Alma, growing pale.

"The same."

"Impossible!"

"But it is the truth."

"How do you know it? It is incredible!"

"Listen! Recently, while returning from the mountain, I met twelve horsemen, clothed in white. At their head was a young man, masked, who appeared to be their chief. It was Bel Demonio and his troop. Suddenly the leader's horse stumbled, whereupon he seized his dagger and roughly struck the animal on the head with its handle. While doing this, one of the ribbons by which the mask was attached became loose, and, as the moonlight fell full upon her face, I recognized Regina!"

Alma clasped her hands, sadly shook her head, as she murmured with emotion:

"Oh, and I loved her so!"

"As did I," said Lucrezia, "but not as much as you, poor child!"

And saying this, she took Alma's hands and pressed them affectionately.

"That is not all," she continued. "I saw her again at Spoleto, where she was passing under the name of Countess Orsini. She was coming out of the theater, attended by Mario. He ascended into her litter, and they returned together to the mountain. That is what I had to say to you; and now, believe me, you must no longer love Mario."

"Mario loves her, then?" asked Alma, who had become pensive.

"Perhaps," replied Lucrezia. "At any rate, she loves Mario, and this is a cause of the greatest danger to you; for this Regina will suffer no obstacle to her wishes, and if you become one, she will have you killed, you may be certain, to remove you from her path."

"Kill me?" exclaimed Alma, astounded.

"Remember! Regina is Bel Demonio!"

"Oh! My God! Is not what I hear a dream, and shall I not soon recover?"

"Promise me one thing," said Lucrezia.

"What is it?" asked the young girl.

"Promise me to no longer love Mario!"

"I? No longer love Mario?"

"Well, try at least to make him cease to love you."

"I will try."

"You may be sure that your life depends on it."

"Say my happiness, rather," said Alma, hiding her face in her hands.

The night was approaching, and a sentinel appeared near where the two women were standing.

"Adieu," said Lucrezia, kissing Alma's hand. "And do not forget what I have come to say to you."

"Am I never to see you again, then?"

"You will see me again soon, please God; but see, there is the patrol, and no one must find me with you. Farewell!"

"Farewell!" sadly responded Alma.

Then, gliding through the trees, Lucrezia disappeared.

This conversation had affected Alma most deeply. She reentered the castle, sad and thoughtful. She had suddenly begun to discover how fleeting are all human hopes.

Moreover, in spite of the revelations made to her by Lucrezia, she felt it to be impossible to tear from her heart her affection for Regina. It is difficult to renounce the friendships of our youth. And Mario! How was it possible for her to believe that he had deceived her? How was it possible for her to renounce the hopes which his love had implanted in her heart? It was impossible!

She went to her chamber, and shut herself in. She had scarcely closed the bolt when she heard somebody knock. She listened, and heard the sound of weeping. It was Marina.

"What do you want?" asked Alma.

"Oh, Mademoiselle, for mercy's sake, open the door!" cried Marina, in a suppliant tone.

Alma told her that she did not require her services, and wished to be alone; but Marina persisted, with so many tears and sobs that her mistress had not the heart to deny her admittance.

She opened the door.

Marina was frightfully pale. Her hair fell in disorder down her cheeks, and was a strange fixedness to her glance.

As soon as the door was opened, she threw herself at Alma's knees.

"Oh, Mademoiselle!" she cried, weeping and embracing the young girl's knees, "Oh, Mademoiselle, pardon me!"

"For what?" asked Alma, surprised.

"Oh, Mademoiselle, I cannot live unless you pardon me!"

"But what am I to pardon you for?"

"Oh, I promised to keep the secret, but my tongue— my cursed tongue!—has caused all my misfortunes."

"How? How?"

"Ah!" said Marina after a moment's silence. "The other day. I spoke too much. You told me to say nothing about your cousin's visit, but I told all about it. It was I, I am certain, who put the soldiers on watch."

"Wretched girl!" said Alma, instinctively starting away from her.

"Oh! Let me die!" continued Marina "But do not reproach me!"

The poor child sobbed as if her heart would break, and Alma could not be stern in the presence of a despair so sincere.

"Rise," she said kindly. "Rise, and do not weep like that. The harm is done now, and your despair, however great, can do no good. I pardon you."

"Oh! Thank you ! Thank you!" cried Marina. "But I will not accept your pardon until I have saved your cousin Mario."

"Saved him?" repeated Alma. And a bitter thought weighed for a moment on her heart. "Saved him?" she said to herself, "to restore him to Regina's love Oh, never!"

But a thought such as this could dwell but a moment in a heart as good and devoted as Alma's.

"Ah, well," she quietly replied, "I will save him. I will give him up to Regina, and I... I... I will sacrifice myself! I will marry the Marquis of Santa Fiore!"

Her heart sank within her, and she burst into tears. Marina, in despair, sought to appease her, repeating incessantly:

"I will save him! I assure you, I will save him!"

"But how?" murmured poor Alma.

"Don't you fear!"

"But tell me how?" asked Alma again.

"I will tell you how," said Marina, visibly embarrassed. "Mademoiselle must know that the corporal, Mustaccio, is in love with me; that he would hang himself for me; and that, by saying a word to him, I could send him to the end of the world. Well, if Mademoiselle allows me, I shall be able in the evening, the day after tomorrow, to contrive that your cousin escapes."

"God tries me cruelly," thought poor Alma.

She stifled a sigh, wiped away the last traces of her tears, and then, turning towards Marina, with a calm and smiling countenance, she said:

"Very well! Let us save him."

"Oh, what happiness it will be!" said Marina, jumping with joy.

"But this time," added Alma, "watch your tongue!"

"Oh, I swear that I will cut it out rather than let it betray me a second time!" replied the little maid, with an air of triumph, which, for moment, threw a pleasant gleam over her countenance.

She then went up to her little room, and dressed herself in an Italian peasant girl's handsomest costume.

In the evening, as she was going to bed, she said to Alma:

"All goes well, Mademoiselle. The corporal—Mustaccio—has completely lost his head. He will not sleep tonight. I have told him that I do not think him as ugly as I once did."

Marina reckoned, upon seeing the corporal on the morrow, and on being to induce him to be unmindful of his duty; but chance thought fit to protect Mustaccio's honor, by arranging that he should be for some days on duty on the ramparts of the fortress.

Poor Marina was in despair at this mischance, and Alma could not hide her anxiety.

In the meantime, Count Ercole's wound had begun to heal, and it was to be feared that, once he was recovered, he would gratify himself by some frightful vengeance on the son of his mortal enemy.

The Marquis of Santa Fiore had twice visited his future father-in-law, and had settled the preliminaries of the proposed alliance.

The day appointed for the nuptials was the following Sunday. Ercole was to return to his residence in Spoleto, and the nuptial *fête* was to be held there. A female relation of the Prince was to do the honors of the palace; for it was impossible that he could, as yet, appear in public.

In two days' time, the move to Spoleto was to be made. Alma found it impossible to sleep, and Marina again began to weep; when at length Corporal Mustaccio, who little suspected how much interest he excited, put an end to the the anxiety of the two girls by returning to the fort.

Marina once more leveled her batteries against him, and began by making poor Mustaccio believe that the tears, the traces of which were still visible on her countenance, had been caused by his prolonged absence.

It only required a hint such as this to make Mustaccio completely lose his head Delighted at the interest the chambermaid seemed to feel for him, he hastened to inform her that henceforth he would not have to leave the castle, since Signor Capitan, who had confidence in him, had appointed him to watch over the prisoner.

Marina jumped with joy at the news, and permitted the corporal to kiss her cheek.

An animated conversation followed, and when the bold corporal eagerly pressed his suit, the young girl promised him her hand on a certain condition. We will not say what this was; but the reader may believe us when we say that Marina paid very dearly for Mario's liberty.

"Ah, Mademoiselle," she said, with a sigh, when she next saw Alma. "When I think that am going to marry such a man as Mustaccio!"

"Life is full of sacrifice," said Alma, sadly.

The little maid made a grimace; but she had promised to save Mario, and she was resolved to keep her promise, whatever it might cost her.

On the following morning, Marina went downstairs for a moment, and speedily returned.

"Mustaccio," she said, "is more ingenious than I thought he was. He has formed his plan. This evening he will give me I give me a soldier's old uniform, and will lead us to the prisoner's cell. As soon as Mademoiselle's cousin shall have put on the mantle and helmet, Mustaccio will lead a patrol outside the fortress, and will post Mario on the parapet, opposite Mademoiselle's windows, so that she may be able to see him depart."

"Oh, dear child!" cried Alma. "You have well repaired your fault!"

"Yes," replied Marina, "but I would much rather not marry the corporal."

When it was evening, Marina procured the packet of clothes and the key to the cell, and also provided herself with a dark lantern.

The two young girls waited until all in the fort had gone to bed, and then, at the hour of eleven, prepared to go on their errand.

Marina took the lamp, gently opened the door and went first, pointing the way to her mistress. Both were greatly agitated, and walked on tip-toe. They descended the turret stairs. When they reached the ground floor, Marina opened a low door, and went down four steps. The girls then traversed a damp corridor, at the end of which they perceived, by the light of a lamp hanging on the wall, Mustaccio, who relieving the tedium of his guard by means of a bottle.

Mustaccio hid his bottle, and, making a military salute, said to Alma

"Make haste, Mademoiselle, you have no time to lose, for the patrol will be round in a quarter of an hour."

At the same time, he drew back the bolt, and opened the door of the cell.

Alma took the lantern from the hands of Marina, whom the corporal held by the sleeve, and entered.

From the time that he been thrown into the dungeon, Mario had never experienced a moment's fear. Life, without the hope of obtaining Alma, offered him but a melancholy prospect, and death seemed to him preferable to an existence passed in eternally regretting a lost love. Mario, however, now found himself under the same roof as Count Ercole's daughter. She had said that she loved him; and he hoped that her love, or at least the remembrance of the friendship which had always existed between them, would induce her to endeavor to him.

When Alma entered, Mario was in a deep sleep, dreaming that his beautiful cousin was still throwing her handkerchief to him as a talisman against harm.

At the sound of the opening of the door, he immediately awoke, and found himself face to face with the young girl.

"Is this a dream?" he cried, passing his hand across his forehead. "Alma! You! Are you here?"

"It is indeed me!" replied Alma, sadly. "I have come to restore you your liberty."

"My liberty?" said Mario. "Is it possible?"

"I was the cause, the innocent cause of your capture, and I have been anxious to repair the ill I have involuntarily done, and to restore you to those who love you— whom you love!"

She pronounced these words with a bitterness which Mario did not catch.

"Oh! You are an angel, Alma!" he cried.

"Hasten, hasten, cousin!" exclaimed Alma. "Throw this mantle over your shoulders, and place this helmet on your head. The man who will conduct you beyond the fort is waiting."

"My God! Have I not time, then, dear Alma, to tell you how grateful I am to you! How much I love you!"

"Do not speak of that, Mario! Time presses. You would not wish me to fall victim on account of what I am now doing?"

"Oh, no!" said Mario, who threw the mantle over his shoulders.

At the same moment, Marina knocked at the door.

"Do you hear?" asked Alma.

"I am ready," replied Mario, eagerly seizing the young girl's trembling hands. "What you have done to-day, Alma, unites us more closely than ever. I go, but only to return speedily to remove you from these cursed walls; and when I return, you will not forget, will you, either my love or yours?"

As he said this, he pressed Alma's hands to his lips; but she started back a step, and gently disengaging her hands from her lover's passionate clasp, said, in a grave, low voice:

"Mario, cruel revelations have been made to me since I last saw you. You are free. Return to the mountain, where another love awaits you; for, tomorrow, I shall be the bride of the Marquis of Santa Fiore!"

Mario uttered a stifled cry at this unexpected news.

But Corporal Mustaccio had already knocked at the door several times; a single moment's delay now might be fatal.

"Go! Go!" said Alma.

Before Mario could recover his presence of mind, the door of the dungeon was opened, and Alma and Marina had slipped away, and he found himself alone with Corporal Mustaccio, who placed an old musket in his hands, saying:

"Follow me!"

Mario allowed himself to be mechanically conducted along, scarcely knowing whether he was awake or he was the sport of some strange hallucination.

In the meantime, Alma and Marina had reached their chamber.

Although the supposed daughter of Count Ercole was profoundly sad, she opened her window and awaited, with intense anxiety, the results of Corporal Mustaccio's promises.

In a few moments, she saw a patrol pass along the ramparts and relieve the sentinel. The new sentinel remained for a moment motionless; but when the patrol had moved off, he threw his helmet, musket, and mantle upon the ground, and, gazing for a moment with an eye full of bitterness at the old castle, went on his way across the valley.

"Thank you! Oh, my God, thank you!" said Alma, sinking to her knees.

Mario was saved.

As for Corporal Mustaccio—to finish with him at once—as he was passing along the courtyard on the following morning, he received from Marina a charitable piece of advice, which wonderfully changed his plans.

The chambermaid informed him that his helmet, mantle, and musket had been found on the grass where they had been left by his prisoner, and recognized as his. She left him to draw his own conclusion from this fact.

Corporal Mustaccio, like a man of good sense, calculated that, possessed as he was of the choice of being either married or hung, it would be better for him to avoid either of them by taking flight.

He gallantly kissed Marina on the neck—the little girl, who was glad to be rid of him so cheaply, making no objection; and then left the fort, to gain the mountain, and to join the first free company he might meet with.

When she saw him depart so rapidly, Marina clasped her hands together, heaved a sigh of satisfaction, and thanked Heaven for having relieved her of so great a misfortune.

IX. The Betrothal

On being informed of his prisoner's escape, the old Count's rage knew no bounds. He bitterly repented not having cut the throat of the son of his old enemy at once; but it was now too late, for Mario was already far away.

Alma, however, remained; and now and then the idea of avenging himself upon her would cross his mind. But his personal interests struggled with his hate, and the poor child's gentleness stayed his arm.

After his initial fit of powerless rage, all his former fears came rushing back to him, and seeing no prospect of any safety for himself, save by means of a marriage between his supposed daughter and the powerful Marquis of Santa Fiore, he set out for Spoleto on the following day, leaving a strong garrison in the last of his fortresses.

On the following evening, the eve of the day on which was to be celebrated the marriage between the Marquis of Santa Fiore and the daughter of old Count Ercole, a splendid ball was given in the halls of the Count's palace, to which had been invited all the ranks of Spoleto.

It seemed as if the Count's Spoleto palace had suddenly awakened, and that some beneficent fairy had touched it with a magic wand. That evening, it looked like an enchanted palace.

The ball commenced at ten o'clock. One of the Marquis of Santa Fiore's relatives did the honors with much dignity and grace.

As for the Marquis, balls and *fêtes* held less attraction for him than the pursuit of wild boars; but he discovered so much charm in the person of his *fiancée* that, for the first time in his life, he did not feel bored at a ball.

However, the same could not be said for poor Alma. Pale, with mournful eyes, she felt as isolated in the midst this crowd of strangers as one who had been shipwrecked in the midst of the vast ocean. A terrible sadness overwhelmed her. The graceful beauty of the ball, and the fresh breezes of the night, failed to please either her heart or her mind; and, resigned to her fate, she no longer attempted struggle against the misery which her overwhelmed her. The sounds of the *fête* reached her ears like a confused murmur, which they did not comprehend, and even the dancing could not distract her thoughts.

Suddenly, two well known forms, gliding through the crowd, passed before her eyes—Mario, with Regina leaning on his arm. A dagger stroke could not have pained the poor child more than did this sight. Regina seemed happy; while everyone pressed around her, addressing her as Countess Orsini.

"You must admit," said Mario, speaking low, "that you have made me commit a very imprudent action—persuading me, as you have done, to enter the house of the man who, two days ago, held me prisoner!"

"Are you frightened, cousin Mario?" asked Regina, in a mocking tone.

"I am frightened of nothing," he replied, "that is, of nothing in the natural order of things; but you impress me with the idea that you are one of those beautiful creatures who, by their smiles, attract knights into snares where they meet their deaths!"

"Unless they submit," said Regina, smiling bitterly.

"And then they are changed into beasts!"

"Whenever you speak of me, my cousin," replied Regina, "you have nothing but evil things to utter!"

Mario did not answer, for just then, he spotted Alma. His countenance became frightfully pale.

"What is the matter?" asked Regina.

Instead of replying, Mario abruptly withdrew his arm, and was lost in the crowd. Then, after having purposely made a circuit for the purpose of deceiving Regina's watchful eye, he approached Alma who lowered her eyes and trembled.

"Is it true, then, Alma?" he asked, in a voice full of emotion, "that you no longer love me?"

Alma at first made no reply, but when Mario repeated his question, she murmured, with difficulty:

"Is it for you, then, to ask me such a question?"

"Oh, dear Alma!" said Mario. "I have never for a single instant ceased to love you!"

"It is too late," replied Alma, shaking her head. "We must no longer speak of the past. See! This is my nuptial *fête*! All is ended between us."

As she uttered these words, she turned any and gave her hand to the Marquis of Santa Fiore, who had come to seek her.

Mario remained fixed to the same spot, his eyes cast on the ground, his mouth half open. Was it rage, despair, or terror? It was love! Mario loved Alma with all the strength of his soul, and he perceived that every instant was deepening the abyss which separated them.

At that moment he felt a tiny hand pressing his arm. He turned, and saw Regina. She again placed her arm under that of her cousin, and without saying a word, made him pass through the gallery and the salons.

With some difficulty they succeeded in escaping from the crowd. One of the garden gates was open, and she led Mario thither. The night was dark. Mario's heart beat vehemently against his breast, and he asked himself what could be Regina's object in having recourse to all this mystery. But Regina remained silent, while she walked quickly, and drew her cousin along with her as if she wished to leave him no time for reflection.

At length, she paused. She made her cousin sit down upon a grassy bank, and seated herself by his side. For a moment they were both so completely silent that the breeze brought to them the faint murmurs of the *fête*.

Mario felt Regina's arm tremble beneath his own.

"Regina," he said, in a voice he endeavored to render firm, "why have you brought me here?"

Regina sighed, but did not answer. Without understanding what was passing in her heart, Mario felt embarrassed.

"Let us go," he suddenly said, making a movement as if he would rise.

"No, remain!" said Regina. "I must speak plainly, since you do not, or will not, understand me. It is better that this discussion should take place immediately; and you, who know me, Mario, will understand how much I have struggled with my pride before I could condescend to the humiliation of asking for this conversation as a favor."

Mario's discomfort increased with every word, for he now realized the purpose of their conversation; and, in the state in which his heart was, it could not but prove embarrassing in the extreme. In the meantime, Regina's voice had lost its usual imperious tone. She no longer ordered; she entreated.

"Mario," she continued, as she let her head lean gently on his shoulder, "Mario! Is it true, then, that you will not love me?"

And then, as Mario did not answer, she added passionately:

"I... I love you! Do you understand? I have long restrained this mad passion which makes my heart so sore; but I have suffered too much, and I have neither the strength nor the will to continue to suffer. Mario! Mario! I love you!"

As she spoke thus, Regina pressed her lips to Mario's, and tenderly clasped his hands in her own. Regina was young and pretty, and, for an instant, Mario's heart beat quickly, and a thrill ran through his body.

"Oh, love me!" continued Regina. "Spare me just a bit of love, Mario—I ask it on my knees; to obtain your love I have rejected all those who have courted me. It is not today that I have begun to love you, ungrateful one! Do you know how many years it has been since my heart has burned with love for you? Oh, answer me! Answer me! Mario, do you love me?"

These incoherent and passionate words filled Mario with the greatest dismay. He would have wished to stop his cousin in her dangerous course, for he perceived that the longer he allowed her to speak, the more difficult it would be to answer her sincerely. But his tongue was glued to his palate.

"You do not answer me," she said, approaching Mario still more closely.

But the evil inclination which had for a moment stirred Mario's heart had already completely receded; the freshness of the evening had calmed his blood, and gently releasing himself from the young girl's embrace, he said to her, sadly and earnestly:

"Regina, listen to me."

"Oh! You do not love me!" exclaimed Regina, dropping down in despair.

Mario repressed a sudden movement of impatience as he lifted her up and made her sit beside him.

"Regina!" he said, "listen to me, I entreat you!"

But Regina scarcely listened, for before he spoke, she knew what he was going to say.

"Speak!" she said at length. "Speak! You see that I have no more strength left. It is not Bel Demonio who is here, or the Countess Orsini, or even the Regina of the mountains; it is only a poor girl who loves and who weeps."

These words were uttered in such a tone of sadness that Mario was deeply touched by them, and tears came to his eyes. There was a moment's silence. The feeble murmurs of the night breeze as it passed through the foliage added still more to the sadness of the scene.

"I wish to speak frankly to you, Regina; and it is for that reason that I entreat you to be a little calm and reasonable," replied Mario, endeavoring to make his manner as serious and earnest as possible. "A love such as yours ought not to be repaid by a mere ordinary affection; and I must confess to you that I do not find in my soul that all-powerful energy, those sublime transports of devotion, which could alone reply properly to a passion so deep as yours. If I allow myself be over persuaded today, how justly you might reproach me at some future time! Oh, how great would be your disenchantment when you awoke from your dream! No, Regina! I love you—yes, I love you with all the sincerity of a loyal and sincere heart; and I am too anxious to preserve your affection for me to run the risk of losing it by cherishing for an instant your present daydream!"

While Mario was speaking, the tears dried on Regina's cheeks. Her expression gradually became lit up by a new flame, and her head, which had been reclining on the young man's breast, lifted up with an air of stern pride.

A smile, tinged with the utmost bitterness, played upon her lips; and she rose fiercely, as she said:

"Enough, Mario enough! Do not add falsehood to insult!"

"What do you mean?" asked Mario, astonished.

"I mean," said Regina, with ill disguised wrath, "that instead of rejecting thus disdainfully the love I offer you, you would have acted more loyally by avowing your love for Alma!"

"Alma?" said Mario.

"Ah!" continued the young girl. "Alma's love is not as extravagant and ridiculous as mine, is it? And you would not have need, to use your own words, of that all-powerful energy, of these sublime transports!"

"Did I say that?" murmured Mario.

"You have said more than that, for you love her!"

"And suppose I do?" asked Andrea's son, now driven to shout.

"You confess it, then?"

"Yes! I do love her!" exclaimed Mario, energetically. "And since you force me to say it, my heart is too full of love for her to allow any other love to occupy it."

Regina listened to this with clenched teeth.

"It is well," she said, with a deep voice. "It is well! But if you see her this evening, Mario, tell Alma that you have pronounced her sentence of death!"

As she uttered these words, Regina broke into a short laugh, and disappeared.

Mario would have followed her, but she was already hidden amidst the trees.

He reentered the palace, but could not find her there. The crowd had, in the meantime, considerably diminished. It was late, and everyone was retiring. Mario, anxious and despairing, was not even able to see Alma, to warn her of the danger which she ran, and was at length compelled to leave with the others.

X. The Fire

The night was already far advanced. There was not a star in the sky. The squares and streets of Spoleto were wrapped in the most profound darkness.

From time to time, some gentleman, preceded by lackeys bearing torches, passed along one of the deserted thoroughfares, and when he had passed, it became once more dark and silent.

The *fête* was at an end in the Vitelli palace. The chandeliers still burned brilliantly at the windows, and from the open doors still issued some of the tardy guests who are never willing to leave either the ball or the gaming table until the light of the sun has dimmed that of the lamps.

The windows of the palace threw weak gleams of light upon the shadowy space which stretched before it.

The torches which had been placed on each side of the Court of Honor went out one by one, and seemed in the night like red points which had been put there for some fantastic reason, rather than for any useful purpose.

A few steps from the Court of Honor, a poor woman crouched in the angle of a wall, indifferent to all that passed around her. She gazed at the palace, and great tears fell from her eyes.

"They are both there," she murmured. "Both young, beautiful, charming. But which is it? Oh, my God! Would that it might be Alma!"

A litter came out of the palace surrounded by torches. The poor woman had recognized Regina in the Countess Orsini; or, in other words, the personage whose

231

name was never pronounced save in an undertone—Bel Demonio!

The group passed like a ray of light across the dark square and disappeared at the corner of a street.

The poor woman sighed.

"Always that Regina!" she said. "I do not know it is, but I fear that some calamity will tonight fall upon her whom I love the most."

Lucrezia Mammone, for it was she who spoke thus, as she uttered these words, buried her face in her hands

"Sixteen years ago," she thought, "I also was young, beautiful, and *fêted*. I also believed that I might be happy in this world, which is so full of misery. But, Oh! If I might only live again in my child"

For some time, she remained with her head hidden in her hands, thinking of the sad past, and of the future which presented so sad a prospect. Suddenly the sound of footsteps on the square made her raise her head. Then she perceived in the darkness twelve men with dark faces and white mantles, advancing towards the Vitelli palace. Regina walked beside them.

Lucrezia recognized her almost immediately.

The twelve men and the young girl stopped close to the entrance of the palace, at a few paces distant from Lucrezia, but the night was so dark that they did not see her.

While she seemed to reckon them with her eyes, Regina said, in that shrill voice which vibrated so well amidst the mountains:

"Will you always be true to me?"

"Until death!" replied the twelve slaves.

"It is well! The hour for you to best prove your devotion has come!" replied the young girl, while her eyes gleamed with fire.

"What are we to do?"

"Listen to me! There are in that palace three persons whom I hate—Ercole Vitelli, the duenna Mercedes, and the *fiancée* of the Marquis of Santa Fiore. Those three must die!"

The Moors bent their heads without uttering a word.

"Six of you," continued Regina, "will place yourselves at the gate of this palace. I have plans for the other six. I myself will enter. A young girl will come out before the end of the night. You will let her pass, for it will be me. But if a second young girl should attempt to leave, kill her without mercy, for she will be my enemy!"

At the rising of the sun, she will no longer exist," replied the slaves.

And forthwith six of the Moors posted themselves at the entrance of the Court of Honor. Three of them concealed themselves behind the pillar on the right, and three behind that on the left. The entrance was large, too large, perhaps, to enable anyone to distinguish the features of a person passing through it, but not so large that anyone standing beside it could not distinguish the age of whoever should pass through it.

When the six Moors had taken up their positions, Regina turned towards the rest of her troop, and said:

"Tonight, you will complete the work of destruction which we have undertaken together. Before an hour has elapsed you will set fire to this palace. I command that, before tomorrow's sunset, not one stone of this royal edifice shall rest upon another. Go!"

And at Regina's imperious gesture, the six slaves retired, each taking a separate path.

In the meantime, Lucrezia, terrified, scarcely dared to breathe.

"Is it," she murmured to herself, "some evil spirit sent by God to punish Ercole and Mercedes for their crimes? No! For God would not involve in such a chastisement that pure child, Alma, who would find pity at the hands of the Devil himself!"

When Regina found herself alone, she threw around her a proud and implacable glance, as she exclaimed:

"Now, let what is fated be fulfilled!"

She walked with a firm step towards the palace.

As she crossed the threshold, Lucrezia Mammone, who had been crouching in the angle of the wall, arose.

"A great crime is about to be committed!" she said. "One of the two victims is my daughter. God must now guide me."

And then she added, repeating Regina's words:

"Let what is fated be fulfilled!"

She also entered the palace.

In the meantime, Regina had reached the galleries. Here and there, the lamps still burned, and the rooms were in the disorder in which they had been left by the ball. Half-faded bouquets strewed the floors, and all about the deserted halls seemed to linger, as it were, some last perfume of the *fête*. Here and there, lackeys slept, stretched upon the sofas; but none of them awoke to oppose Regina's passage.

For some time she wandered at hazard, from apartment to apartment, throughout the vast palace. Like some demon of vengeance she went, with pale face, clenched teeth, and gleaming eyes, searching in vain on all sides for her prey.

At length, she reached a little salon which seemed to have but one point of ingress or egress.

She carefully opened the door, and stretched forth her head in the manner of a serpent that glides between two branches.

She perceived a small chamber hung with blue tapestry, and lit by an alabaster lamp. Alma, seated on an ottoman, her eyes half-closed, and her arms languid with sleep, was making her *toilette* for the night, and playing carelessly with the heavy locks of her abundant hair.

At the sound made by the opening of the door, Alma turned quickly, and uttered a slight cry.

"Regina!' she exclaimed, in a tone of mingled pleasure and surprise.

Then, without a moment's hesitation, she gently stretched out her arms towards her.

Regina hesitated a moment; but those two blue eyes, those white arms, that ineffable gentleness, which disarmed everyone that came within its influence, was all-powerful over Ercole's daughter. She felt her animosity fading away; her angry eyes grew soft, and, vanquished by Alma's touching appeal, so full of candor and innocence, she ran and threw herself into her arms.

The two embraced, as they had done in the happy times of their childhood, with frankness and affection.

"Oh, I was sure that you would come," said Alma, after a moment's silence.

The utmost pleasure sparkled in the poor child's eyes. She was so naive and pure that suspicion could not enter her heart. She spoke to Regina of her past life in the mountain, of Andrea, of Ercole, and of Mario. She recalled the happy days they had passed together, and only paused when fatigue weighed down her eyes, and she felt slumber creeping over her limbs.

It was very late, and Regina, also oppressed with weariness, could scarcely articulate. Gradually and almost insensibly, the words fell from their lips at longer intervals; and their eyes—brilliant stars concealed by the vapors of sleep—closed. Alma laid her beautiful but weary head on her sister's shoulder, and they were both soon buried in a profound slumber.

They slept peacefully beneath the chaste rays of the alabaster lamp, locked in each other's arms, as on that terrible night when Andrea, having entered their chamber, and not knowing which to choose, had seized them both. A strange circumstance suddenly rendered the position precisely similar.

Meanwhile, Lucrezia Mammone, having wandered in vain throughout the palace, which was wrapped in as universal a slumber as a palace in a fairy story, had at length arrived at Alma's chamber.

She entered gently and saw the two young girls asleep. She could scarcely believe her eyes after the words she had heard uttered by Regina. She paused on the threshold, pale, astonished, undecided, asking herself whether she were not the victim of some fatal hallucination.

At that moment, however, the first hollow and menacing murmurs of a conflagration made themselves heard, and already the flames, climbing up the exterior walls, threw over the edifice their sinister, gleaming red light.

The poor mother remained motionless for a moment, contemplating, with a perplexity impossible to describe, the charming sight of the two young girls.

"I can save but one of them. Inspire me then, O God! Tell me which one is my child!"

The moments were precious. Cries began to be heard in the distance; the fire was gradually gaining ground. Lucrezia ran to the window; she saw the flames twisting around the angles of the palace, creeping up the roof, and mounting towards the sky.

"Which one? Oh, my God! Which one?" she exclaimed, returning to gaze again at the two girls.

For a moment, the sound of her voice awakened Regina. She opened her eyes and, seeing the poor woman standing in front of the ottoman, she turned away, murmuring in a tone of aversion:

"Lucrezia Mammone!"

Then she again fell asleep; but her head, as it fell, heavy with slumber, struck Alma's bosom, and awakened her in her turn.

"Lucrezia Mammone!" she exclaimed, as she perceived the latter.

At the same time, she stretched out her arms in so caressing a manner that the poor woman, suddenly enlightened by maternal instinct, threw herself towards Alma.

"It is she! It is she!" she cried, seizing her in her arms.

She lifted her from ottoman, and Alma, still half asleep, allowed herself to be treated like a child.

The powerful instinct of maternity suddenly developed Lucrezia's courage. She felt a supernatural strength in all her limbs, and swiftly carried her daughter across the galleries without looking back.

Regina, overcome by fatigue, and a thousand conflicting emotions, still slept.

While she ran, Lucrezia from time to time covered her daughter's forehead with ardent kisses.

"Fly, fly!" she said.

"I shall have twice owed my life to you!" said Alma, as she stepped on the threshold of the palace.

The two women traversed the Court of Honor. It was a terrible moment for Lucrezia; her heart almost stood still.

But the dark followers of Bel Demonio, concealed behind the pillars, did not show themselves, for they had been told to let the first young girl pass.

"Saved! My daughter is saved!" cried Lucrezia, falling to her knees on the pavement of the square.

She clasped her daughter in an embrace which, this time, was a happiness free from all doubt.

In the meantime, the flames advanced with incredible rapidity, and the palace could only be seen through a glowing veil of fire, smoke, and burning ashes. The beams cracked under the devouring action of the fire, and the rock on which the palace stood was illumined by a broad blood-red light.

When Regina awoke, she perceived the progress of the fire, and saw that she was alone in the midst of the apartment. She uttered a terrible cry.

"Alma!" she cried, seeking her victim on all sides.

There was no reply. She ran to the window. The palace was enveloped in flames. She became frightfully pale.

Suddenly terrible cries proceeded from a neighboring chamber. The door was violently thrown open, and an old man and woman threw themselves into the chamber in which Regina stood. The flames pursued them, hissing like enraged serpents. The old man was in the extremest terror, and could scarcely support himself on his trembling legs. The old woman was pale with fright. They were Ercole Vitelli and Mercedes.

"Regina!" cried the old man, as he entered. "My daughter! Oh, in what a moment do I find you!"

"I am Bel Demonio, thine enemy!"

"You are my daughter! My daughter!"

"It is I who have ruined you!"

"I have nothing but you in all the world!"

"It is I who have set fire to your palace. I am not your daughter, and I detest you as my enemy!"

"God is exacting his vengeance!" cried Mercedes.

"Let us fly," said the old man, who perceived the flames surrounding them with an impenetrable circle.

"It is the gate of Hell!" cackled Mercedes.

"It was you who helped me to commit the murder!" shouted the old man. "You are a wretch!"

"My God, have mercy upon us!"

"Ah!" said Regina, "you are the assassins! Die, then, in expiation of your crimes!"

The flames were approaching.

Regina ran to the window, opened it violently, and threw herself into the Court.

She had scarcely touched the ground when the ceiling of the chamber fell in with a terrible crash, and buried Mercedes and the old Count in the midst of the flames.

The flames leaped to the Heavens with strange and fearful noise.

Regina, filled with terror, rose and ran to the opening of the Court.

The night was drawing to a close. The first rays of dawn were already mingling with the light of the conflagration.

Regina saw from afar, in the midst of the square, a group abounding in love and happiness, the members of which, with uplifted eyes, seemed to be thanking God.

This group was composed of Alma, of Mario, of Lucrezia Mammone, and Andrea Vitelli.

A cry of rage escaped from Regina's breast.

Fury and terror hastened her steps. She had already reached the threshold of the Court, when six black men in white mantles, suddenly sprang from behind the columns and fell upon her, swords in hand.

"Stop!" she cried "I am Bel Demonio!"

But before she had finished, she fell, struck by the simultaneous blows of the six fearsome Moors.

Afterword
Whither the Vitellis?

When Paul Féval wrote *The Companions of the Silence* in 1857 (also available from Black Coat Press), seven years had passed since he had penned *Bel Demonio*, a much shorter work, which had first run in serial form in *Le Pays*.

One wonders if *Bel Demonio* wasn't cut short at the editor's request because it wasn't popular enough amongst the readers, or if Féval was distracted by his other, far more successful work, *La Fée des Grèves* [The Fairy of the Sands],which he was writing at roughly the same time.

In any event, *Bel Demonio* feels somewhat rushed, with a hurried conclusion that doesn't even bother to spell out the consequences of its alleged happy ending. Will Andrea Vitelli, despite being a brigand for all those years, be restored as the rightful heir of the Monteleone family? Will Mario and Alma finally wed? What of Lucrezia's fate? And what of Fiamma, Count Ercole's other daughter?

Seven years later, Féval embarked on a very different story with *The Companions of the Silence*, but for unknown reasons—perhaps sentimental ones?—he felt the need to write a sequel to the much afflicted Monteleone family, as well as create a new Bel Demonio.

We can safely assume that the Mario Monteleone who is one of the main protagonists of *The Companions of the Silence* is a descendent, four or five times removed,[21] of Mario and Alma, who obviously regained the family name, titles and estate. Presumably the Christian name of Mario is still honored in the family by conferring it upon its male descendents.

In *The Companions of the Silence*, one of Mario's sons, Fulvio Coriolani, eventually decides to become a brigand leader and adopts the *nom-de-guerre* of Bel Demonio. To the extent that in *Bel Demonio*, Andrea is already calling himself "Demonio," and it is Regina, a girl, who uses the sobriquet of "Bel Demonio," this is a little surprising, but one might assume that, with the passing of time, either of those two terms have become the traditional name for the brigand leader of the region.

Where Féval throws us a curve ball is in *The Companions of the Treasure* (1870-72), when he reveals that the children of the Mario Monteleone from *The Companions of the Silence* may well be, if not the direct grandchildren of the sinister Colonel Bozzo-Corona, leader of the Black Coats, but at least his descendents.[22] One could theorize that Mario's mother may have had an affair with the Colonel, but that doesn't seem very romantic.

According to Féval, the Colonel is Michele Bozzo (or Pozzo), a bandit once known as Fra Diavolo. He was born in Bastia, in 1722 or 1739 (Féval's chronology is

---

[21] The Mario Monteleone of *The Companions of the Silence* would have been born in the early 1770s.

[22] For more on the continuity problems created by Mario's grandchildren, see our Afterword to the Black Coat Press edition of *The Companions of the Silence*

uncertain about this point) and eventually became the leader of a crime family called the "Brothers of La Merci," based in Sartene, connected to other crime families, such as the Reni of Sartene, the Coronas of Bastia, the Gioja of Naples, etc.

Rather than believing that the Colonel is a descendent of Mario and Alma, we prefer to think that he is descended from Fiamma Vitelli, Ercole's eldest daughter, conveniently forgotten at the conclusion of *Bel Demonio*.

The enmity that existed first between Francis and Ercole Vitelli, then between Andrea and Ercole, eventually continued through their descendents, and it is therefore no surprise that Michele Bozzo, a.k.a. Fra Diavolo, a descendent of Ercole Vitelli, would have found himself naturally opposed to Mario Monteleone, a descendent of Andrea Vitelli.

Jean-Marc Lofficier

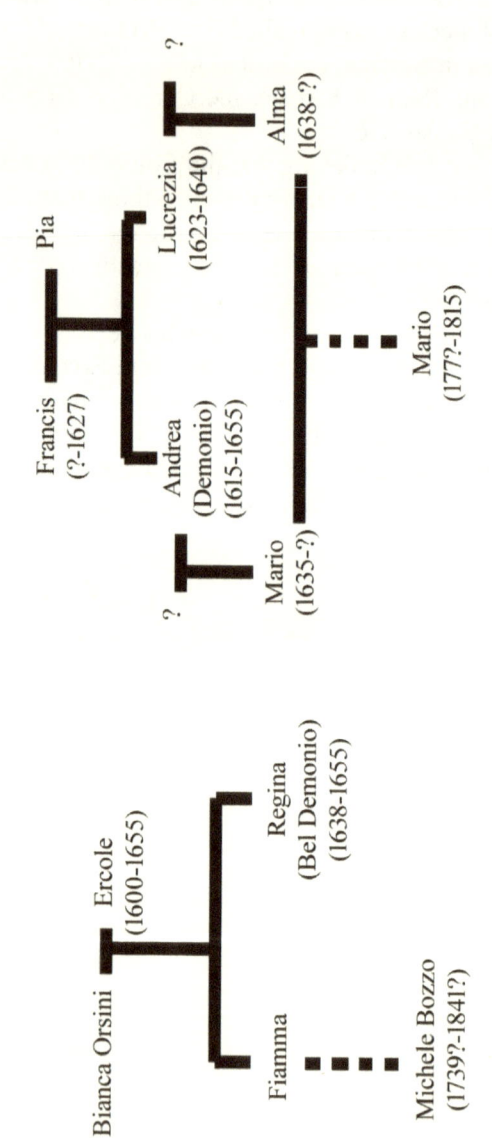

MYSTERIES & THRILLERS

M. Allain & P. Souvestre. *The Daughter of Fantômas; The Death of Fantômas*

A. Anicet-Bourgeois & Lucien Dabril. *Rocambole* (stage plays)

Guy d'Armen. *Doc Ardan: The City of Gold and Lepers; The Troglodytes of Mount Everest/The Giants of Black Lake; The Abominable Snowman*

A. Bernède. *Belphegor*; *Judex* (w/Louis Feuillade); *The Return of Judex* (w/Louis Feuillade); *The Shadow of Judex* (anthology)

A. Bisson & G. Livet. *Nick Carter vs. Fantômas* (stage play)

André Caroff. *The Terror of Madame Atomos; Miss Atomos; The Return of Madame Atomos; The Mistake of Madame Atomos; The Monsters of Madame Atomos; The Revenge of Madame Atomos; The Resurrection of Madame Atomos; The Mark of Madame Atomos; The Spheres of Madame Atomos; The Wrath of Madame Atomos* (w/M. & Sylvie Stéphan); *The Sins of Madame Atomos* (w/M. & Sylvie Stéphan)

Félicien Champsaur. *Homo-Deus; Nora, The Ape-Woman; Ouha, King of the Apes*

Jules Clarétie. *Obsession*

V. Darlay & H. de Gorsse. *Arsène Lupin vs. Sherlock Holmes: The Stage Play* (stage play)

Harry Dickson. *Harry Dickson: The Heir of Dracula; Harry Dickson vs. The Spider*

Séamas Duffy. *Sherlock Holmes in Paris*

Paul Féval. *The Black Coats (The Parisian Jungle; Heart of Steel; The Sword-Swallower; 'Salem Street; The Invisible Weapon; The Companions of the Treasure; The Cadet Gang); The Companions of the Silence; Gentlemen of the Night; John Devil*

Paul Féval, *fils. Felifax, the Tiger-Man*

Louis Forest. *Someone is Stealing Children in Paris*

Fortuné du Boisgobey: *Two Crimes*

Émile Gaboriau. *Monsieur Lecoq; The Casebook of Monsieur Lecoq*

Arnould Galopin: *Harry Dickson: The Man in Grey; Tenebras*

Goron & Émile Gautier. *Spawn of the Penitentiary*

G.L. Gick. *Harry Dickson: The Werewolf of Rutherford Grange*

Léon Gozlan. *The Vampire of the Val-de-Grâce*

Georges Grison. *The Heads that fell in Paris* (non-fiction)

Paul d'Ivoi. *Around the World on Five Sous* (w/Henri Chabrillat)

Paul Lacroix. *Danse Macabre*

Jean de La Hire. *Enter the Nyctalope; The Nyctalope on Mars; The Nyctalope vs. Lucifer; The Nyctalope Steps In; Night of the Nyctalope; Return of the Nyctalope*

Rick Lai. *Shadows of the Opera: Retribution in Blood; Sisters of the Shadows: The Curse of Cagliostro*

Etienne-Léon de Lamothe-Langon. *The Virgin Vampire*

Steve Leadley. *Sherlock Holmes and The Circle of Blood*

Maurice Leblanc. *Arsène Lupin vs. Countess Cagliostro; Arsène Lupin vs. Sherlock Holmes: 1. The Blonde Phantom; 2. The Hollow Needle; The Island of the Thirty Coffin; 813; The Many Faces of Arsène Lupin* (anthology)

Gustave Lerouge: *The Mysterious Doctor Cornelius* (3 vols.)

Gaston Leroux. *Chéri-Bibi* (stage play)*; The Phantom of the Opera; Rouletabille & the Mystery of the Yellow Room; Rouletabille at Krupp's*

Maurice Limat. *Mephista*

Jean-Marc & Randy Lofficier. *The Katrina Protocol;* (anthologists) *Tales of the Shadowmen 1-13; The Vampire Almanac* (2 vols.)

Charles Malato. *Lost!*

Richard Marsh. *The Complete Adventures of Judith Lee*

William Patrick Maynard. *The Terror of Fu Manchu; The Destiny of Fu Manchu*

Frank J. Morlok. *Sherlock Holmes: The Grand Horizontals* (stage play)*; Sherlock Holmes vs Jack the Ripper* (stage play);

Sherlock Holmes, Fantômas, Lupin, Raffles and More: The Spanish Plays (stage plays)

Jean Petithuguenin. *The Adventures of Ethel King, The Female Nick Carter*

P.-A. Ponson du Terrail. *The Immortal Woman; The Vampire and the Devil's Son; The Police Agent*

Georges Price. *The Missing Men of the* Sirius

Charles Rabou: *The Secret Bureau: The Secret Bureau: The Brothers of Death*

Antonin Reschal. *The Adventures of Miss Boston, The First Female Detective*

Henri de Saint-Georges. *The Green Eyes*

Norbert Sevestre. *Sâr Dubnotal: Jack the Ripper; The Astral Trail*

Eugène Thébault. *Radio-Terror*

P. de Wattyne & Y. Walter. *Sherlock Holmes vs. Fantômas* (stage play)

David White. *Fantômas in America*

Pierre Yrondy. *The Adventures of Thérèse Arnaud of the French Secret Service; The Adventures of Marius Pégomas, Marseille Detective*